TWENTY-ONE TRUTHS

ABOUT LOVE

ALSO BY MATTHEW DICKS

FICTION
Something Missing
Unexpectedly, Milo
Memoirs of an Imaginary Friend
The Perfect Comeback of Caroline Jacobs

NONFICTION
Storyworthy

TWENTY-ONE TRUTHS

ABOUT LOVE

Matthew Dicks

St. Martin's Press New York

First published in the United States by St. Martin's Press, an imprint of St. Martin's Publishing Group

TWENTY-ONE TRUTHS ABOUT LOVE. Copyright © 2019 by Matthew Dicks. All rights reserved. Printed in the United States of America. For information, address St. Martin's Publishing Group, 120 Broadway, New York, NY 10271.

Lyrics from "Code Monkey" copyright © 2006 by Jonathan Coulton

www.stmartins.com

Designed by Devan Norman

The Library of Congress Cataloging-in-Publication Data is available upon request.

ISBN 978-1-250-10348-2 (hardcover)
ISBN 978-1-250-10349-9 (ebook)

Our books may be purchased in bulk for promotional, educational, or business use. Please contact your local bookseller or the Macmillan Corporate and Premium Sales Department at 1-800-221-7945, extension 5442, or by email at MacmillanSpecialMarkets@macmillan.com.

First Edition: November 2019

10 9 8 7 6 5 4 3 2 1

FOR SHEP,
WHO ALWAYS GETS IT,
EVEN WHEN IT'S POSSIBLY
JUST HIM AND ME

ACKNOWLEDGMENTS

Boundless thanks to the following people for making this book possible:

My wife, Elysha, who I write for first and foremost, even when she's not reading my stuff on a timely basis (*or at all*).

My in-laws, Barbara and Gerry Green, for continuing to fill my life with their enthusiasm, excitement, and unsolicited counsel. About once a month, Gerry will say, "Tell me something exciting, Matt! Give me some news!" He has no idea how long I have waited for someone to ask me questions like that.

Matthew Shepard, who remains my first reader and the person who always sees what others do not.

My brother, Jeremy, who offered a solution to a sticking point in this book that threatened to derail the whole damn thing. I might still be trying to get unstuck if not for his brilliant suggestion, offered while sitting in section 331 of Gillette Stadium, watching the Patriots win another game alongside me.

Donna Gosk and Amy Doherty, who read these lists before they were even a novel, when professional development seminars were proving to be less than professional and hardly developmental. My attempts to make them laugh with amusing bits of nonsense unexpectedly resulted in this story.

Steve Brouse, who allowed himself to unknowingly be co-opted as a character for this novel and not protesting after the fact. He is exactly as he is portrayed in this novel: brilliant, bold, and unwaveringly ethical beyond compare.

All of my friends who graciously read the early drafts of this book and told me when I was being obtuse, confusing, and tragically unamusing. Your untempered, hurtful words have helped to make this book so much better.

Kaitlin Severini, my copy editor, who has not only spared me many a literary embarrassment but has gone above and beyond the call of duty researching, confirming, and correcting multiple bits of nonfiction references in this book and correcting my math again and again. The job of a copy editor knows no bounds. They are truly the Swiss Army knives of the literary world, and I'm so pleased that Kaitlin Severini was so sharp.

NaNá Stoelzle, the proofreader of the final text of this book. As a perfectionist, even the smallest error makes me lose my mind. Knowing that a professional perfectionist read every line of this book allows me to sleep well at night.

Every person who told me with absolute certainty that a bunch of lists could never tell a story. I love it when people tell me what I can't do, and I love saying, "I told you so" even more.

Hannah Braaten, my editor and coconspirator, who rescued this book from the hinterland and carried it to the mountaintop. I feel so very fortunate to have found someone so talented and so skilled to shepherd my work from scratches and scribbles to a real life book.

Lastly, thanks to Taryn Fagerness, my agent, friend, and partner in this creative life. She found me in the slush pile years ago and changed my life forever. She makes my sentences better, my stories better, and as a result, my life better. It's not often that another human being can make your dreams come true, but she did, and I am forever thankful.

NOVEMBER

NOVEMBER 1
8:15 PM

Ways to keep Jill from getting pregnant
1. Refuse to have sex
2. Fake orgasms
3. Wear a condom without her knowledge
4. Get a vasectomy without her knowledge

Realistic ways to keep Jill from getting pregnant
1. Fake orgasms
2.

NOVEMBER 2
6:00 AM

Finances
Savings: 11,562

Income
What I tell Jill: 1,800
Reality: 773
Jill: 2,900

Expenses
> Mortgage: 2,206
> Toyota: 276
> Honda: 318
> Car insurance: 175
> Student loans: 395
> Cable and Internet: 215
> Electric: 85
> Oil: 775! (WTF?)
> Phones: 180
> Gas: 120
> Other stuff: Too much

Number of months before we run out of money
> 9

Number of months before Jill thinks we will run out of money
> Never

Number of minutes per hour that I worry about running out of money
> 52 (approximately)

NOVEMBER 4
6:00 AM

DAYS WITHOUT

Chocolate glazed doughnuts	443
Gum	12

Crying	19
Little Debbie Snack Cakes	1
Green vegetables	9
Flossing	0
Retail rage	3
Regret over quitting my job	0
Dad	5,647

NOVEMBER 4
8:10 AM

5 Problems with Lying
1. We lie most often to the people we love.
2. There is no greater shame than getting caught in a lie.
3. A lie often requires additional lies, making it impossible to ever come clean.
4. Liars are the worst human beings.
5. Lies always cover up the worst parts of you.

NOVEMBER 4
8:40 AM

How liars with the best intentions are like the owners of every iteration of Jurassic Park
They never set out to hurt anyone.
They operate with enormous hubris.
Denial both perpetuates and intensifies the problem.
The situation inevitably gets worse and worse as time goes by.
The end is never pretty.

Serious question about all Jurassic Park movies
> Why not create only plant-eating dinosaurs? Are brontosauruses and stegosauruses really not exciting enough?

How the brontosaurus is like purgatory
> The brontosaurus was a dinosaur, then it wasn't a dinosaur, but now it might be a dinosaur after all.

NOVEMBER 4
9:30 AM

A New Chapter Picks of the Month for November
> *Treasure Island* by Robert Louis Stevenson (Jim Hawkins was the John McClane of his day)
> *Ready Player One* by Ernest Cline (Ernest Cline apparently lives in my teenage brain)
> *Open: An Autobiography* by Andre Agassi
> *World War Z* by Max Brooks
> *Ballistics: Poems* by Billy Collins

Preferred Choice of Name for Billy Collins (best to worst)
> Billy Collins
> Will Collins
> Bill Collins
> William Collins
> Willy Collins

Preferred Choice of Name for Me (best to worst)
Dan Mayrock
Daniel Mayrock
ANYTHING ELSE
Danny Mayrock

Nicknames for William that the Internet says are real but are not
Liam
Wills
Wylie

NOVEMBER 5
11:30 AM

Einstein's Conditions Upon Which He Agreed to Remain Married to His Wife for the Sake of the Children

CONDITIONS

A. You will make sure:
   1. that my clothes and laundry are kept in good order;
   2. that I will receive my three meals regularly *in my room*;
   3. that my bedroom and study are kept neat, and especially that my desk is left for *my use only*.
B. You will renounce all personal relations with me insofar as they are not completely necessary for social reasons. Specifically, You will forego:
   1. my sitting at home with you;
   2. my going out or travelling with you.

C. You will obey the following points in your relations with me:
    1. you will not expect any intimacy from me, nor will you reproach me in any way;
    2. you will stop talking to me if I request it;
    3. you will leave my bedroom or study immediately without protest if I request it.
D. You will undertake not to belittle me in front of our children, either through words or behavior.

Conditions Upon Which I Will Agree to Remain Married to Jill (also a real list)

CONDITIONS

A. You will allow me to continue to be your husband.
B. You won't kill me in my sleep.

Cosmopolitan and Sex

Number of times I've seen a *Cosmo* cover advertising an article featuring triple-digit sex tips: 9

Number of times I've been tempted to purchase one of these magazines for the sex tips: 9

Number of times I've bought one of these magazines for the sex tips: 3

Total number of sex tips in combined magazines that I have purchased: 304

Total number of useful sex tips: 1

Total number of useful sex tips in Jill's opinion: 0

NOVEMBER 6
4:20 PM

Text messages from Jill at lunchtime

> I wish Jasper wasn't so stupid. How do idiots become principals?
>
> The usual stupid stuff. Can't keep his lies straight. Selfish assholery.
>
> You're lucky you escaped this place.
>
> I miss you being here. I liked seeing you during the day.
>
> No, I'm fine. Stay there. Sell books.
>
> Seriously, I'm good. I have Julie and Lisa and tomato soup.
>
> Can you pick up dog food on the way home from the store? Blue Buffalo.
>
> I don't want to hear it. Clarence deserves the best.
>
> The size of gummy worms compared to the size of gummy bears makes me question the whole gummy universe.
>
> Love you more.

NOVEMBER 8
11:00 AM

Proof that I am stupid

- When I was a kid, I dropped my cotton candy on the ground and tried to wash it off with the hose.
- When I was *in high school*, I still couldn't understand why "a quarter past the hour" wasn't 25 minutes past the hour, because a quarter is 25 cents.
- I always mop myself into the corner of a room.

- I once asked a police officer (in all sincerity) how she would handcuff a one-armed suspect.
- I thought that women had prostates until very, very recently.
- When I was a little kid, I thought that actors actually died in real life when they filmed death scenes for movies, so I was afraid to watch anything but cartoons.
- I only found out recently that a pickle is a desecrated cucumber.
- I didn't realize that fruit juice was loaded with calories until I had gained 20 pounds.
- When I was in Mrs. Lavern's third-grade class, I explained to my classmates that a new moon was when the moon goes away and is replaced by an entirely new moon. Then I tried to pretend like I was joking even though everyone knew that I wasn't. Then I started crying.

NOVEMBER 10
9:10 AM

5 years of Jill
   Sat beside Jill in first faculty meeting
   Made Jill laugh in first faculty meeting
   Fell in love with Jill at first faculty meeting
   Pined over Jill while she dated fucking Feeney
   Waited inappropriate amount of time after breakup with
      Feeney (3 days)

Dated Jill
Learned about Peter
Wondered if I could date a widow
Realized I was being stupid
Wondered if I was being stupid
One-year anniversary at Niagara Falls cheap motel
Dumped by Jill
23 days of hell
Dated Jill again
Moved in with Jill
Proposed to Jill on our second anniversary
Admit to never wanting children "never, ever, ever"
Negotiation (fight) over children
"The 72 Hours of Silence"
Concession (Jill would say "agreement") over children
Negotiation over religion of children
Second thoughts (me, but maybe [probably] Jill, too)
Called off engagement (in my mind only)
Second thoughts a second time
Ice-cold feet
Married
Bought house on Magnolia Hill
One-year wedding anniversary in Kennebunkport, Maine
Quit teaching
Opened bookstore
Failed renegotiation over children
Attempted baby making
Fake orgasms

NOVEMBER 12
8:30 AM

Solutions to pending financial disaster
- Second job (what? when? how would I explain it to Jill?)
- Lottery
- Write a novel (can you actually make money doing this?)
- Day-trading (Do I need money to start?) (Is it a thing?)
- Poker
- Thank-you note idea
- Write to millionaires

Realistic but impossible solutions to pending financial disaster
- Admit to Jill that I'm a failure (this would not actually solve the problem)
- Ask Mom for a loan
- Ask Jake for a loan
- Find an investor for a marginally profitable bookstore

Best but still impossible solutions
- Make the bookstore more profitable

Best solutions if I had a time machine
- Un-quit my teaching position
- Don't open the bookstore
- Don't allow 13 months of denial and lies to pile up while our savings account disappears before thinking about telling Jill

Ways of making the bookstore more profitable
    Sell more books
    Charge more for books
    Negotiate a lower rent
    Lay off employees

Preferred order of layoffs (in an ideal world)
    Kimberly
    Sharon
    Amy
    Jenny
    Steve

Realistic order of layoffs (in a world where I'm afraid of a certain employee)
    Sharon
    Jenny
    Amy
    Steve
    Kimberly

NOVEMBER 15
5:40 AM

Shopping List
    Special K (no fake strawberries)
    Dog food
    AA batteries
    Extra-chunky peanut butter

Little Debbie Snack Cakes
Day Trading for Dummies
Poker for Dummies
Tulips
Kettle ball
Powerball ticket
Birthday present for Mom

NOVEMBER 15
7:50 PM

Things that exist that I didn't think existed
Day Trading for Dummies

Things that don't exist that I thought did
- Kettle balls
- A way of explaining to a muscular salesperson why you
  thought a kettlebell was called a "kettle ball" without
  sounding stupid or slightly perverted

NOVEMBER 15
10:30 PM

Division of Labor
JILL:
Shops for food and most household goods
Cooks almost all meals (doesn't like my cooking)
Sweeps (so she claims)
Washes, folds, and never fucking puts the laundry away

Weeds flower beds
Changes sheets
Walks and feeds Clarence
Cleans bathrooms

DAN:
Pays bills
Brings out trash
Replaces trash bag after taking out trash (which is an additional chore no matter what Jill says)
Definitely sweeps
Washes, folds, and PUTS AWAY LAUNDRY
Ruins Jill's sweaters and jeans while trying to wash them
Mows lawn
Organizes Jill's sink-top cream/lotion/soaps/makeup paraphernalia when she's not looking
Constantly turns off lights (yes, this is a chore)
Cleans out refrigerator
Shovels snow
Rakes leaves into meaningless piles that eventually blow into the neighbor's yard
Processes mail (also a significant chore no matter what Jill says)
Brings trash and recycling to curb on Mondays

Chores I know Peter did because Jill told me
Cooked
Paid bills
Walked and fed Clarence
"Just fixed things when they broke. He was good with that stuff."

Chores I know Peter did because of what Jill didn't tell me but told me anyway

> Took away all of Jill's worries about money, mortgage payments, insurance, retirement planning, broken dishwashers, service contracts, gutter cleaning, flat tires, refinancing, and clogged drains so she could focus on herself and her career

NOVEMBER 16
6:15 PM

Things that people have said to me this week that I don't understand

> "That pass-interference call in the end zone was bullshit."
>
> "Something something something IPO really took off."
>
> "This is clog weather."
>
> "The mill rate in this town is ridiculous."
>
> "You realize you're playing Nickelback. Right?"
>
> "You'd only last about two days on *Naked and Afraid*."
>
> "What's up, *jabroni*?"

NOVEMBER 16
9:25 PM

Problems with being the boss

> Kimberly thinks she's the boss.
>
> Steve should be the boss.
>
> I never wanted to be a boss.

NOVEMBER 16
10:05 PM

My original vision of a bookstore owner
    Read good books
    Recommend good books to smart people
    Dine with authors
    Be rumored to be working on a novel

What being a bookstore owner actually looked like today
    Basic accounting on an Excel spreadsheet that I don't fully
        understand
    Asking three teenage girls if they could please not vape in
        the store
    Finding books for customers based upon color, size, and
        cover art
    Removing a half-eaten muffin from between two Nelson
        DeMille novels
    Telling customers over the phone when we close
    A hell of a lot of vacuuming

NOVEMBER 17
5:35 AM

Things I'm opposed to that I wish I wasn't
    Public nudity (mine only)

Changes I would make to my appearance (in order of importance)
    Back hair
    Lose 20 pounds
    Lose 10 more pounds
    Full head of hair
    Smaller ears
    Six inches taller
    Replace missing pinkie toe
    Neck mole
    Eliminate hair on the tops of my toes
    Whiten teeth

Items left off this list because I can't put them on the list
    Penis

NOVEMBER 17
11:45 AM

Problems with my penis
    I honestly don't know how it compares to other penises when
        erect except for porn penises, which I pray to God are
        not normally sized penises.
    I don't know how large a penis needs to be in order to be a
        satisfactory penis.
    I don't know if different women have different definitions
        of a satisfactory penis size.
    I can't trim or shave my pubic hair because that would im-
        ply that I care when I really shouldn't unless Jill cares
        but I don't know if Jill cares.

NOVEMBER 19
3:30 PM

Reasons I quit teaching
- Kids didn't love me
- Teachers didn't like me
- Principal hated me
- Couldn't continue to witness bad decisions at the expense of children
- Couldn't stand one more minute of professional development that was neither professional nor developmental
- Couldn't stand reading bad writing

Real reasons I quit teaching
- I wasn't a good enough teacher
- It hurt my heart to watch kids waste so much time and ability

Reasons I became a teacher
- Understood the job
- Dad suggested it
- Always liked school
- Mr. Sullivan
- Summer vacations

Teaching revelations
1. Teaching is the only profession that you spend at least 15 years observing before trying to do it yourself.
2. I wouldn't be a teacher if Dad hadn't suggested it.

3. I still think of myself as a teacher even though I'm not.
4. There will always be too many kids in need of saving.
5. If the only reason I became a teacher was for the summer vacations, that would've still be reason enough.

Reasons I opened bookstore
  Love reading good books
  Love browsing bookstores
  Thought it would be easy

Stupidest thought I've ever had
  Owning and operating a bookstore would be easy

Hardest thing about owning and operating a bookstore
  Everything.
  Also . . .
  Making a profit
  Managing employees
  Explaining to employees (employee) that proselytizing to customers is not okay
  Watching great books go unread and terrible books sell like hotcakes
  Reshelving magazines
  Teenagers

NOVEMBER 19
8:50 PM

60 Minutes/Vanity Fair poll of women given a choice of 6 things
to change about their man
    His temper (29 percent)
    His friends (11 percent)
    His mother (9 percent)
    His sense of humor (8 percent)
    His physique (7 percent)
    His hygiene (2 percent)

Jill's comments about this poll
- "*Their man?* Seriously? How old is this poll? Or better, how old are the pollsters?"
- "*60 Minutes* and *Vanity Fair* are bizarre bedfellows."
- "If you need to change your husband's temper, you need to change your husband."
- "Does changing your husband's sense of humor mean giving your husband a sense of humor or fixing the one he already has?"
- "I can just hear it: 'You're leaning a little Seinfeld. I'd really like a little more Bill Hicks, with maybe a dash of Attell.'"
- "I guess if I had to choose, I'd change your mother, but more for your sake than mine."
- "Those numbers only add up to 66%. Where the hell are the other 34%?"

My thoughts on Jill's comments

- She didn't want to change my physique. Or more correctly, she didn't list changing my physique in first position. I silently cheered inside until self-doubt overwhelmed me and I wondered if she was just holding back and trying not to hurt my feelings. Then I felt bad that my wife doesn't like the way I look and is forced to pretend that she does for my own sake. All of this happened in less than a second.
- Who are these men with tempers, and what the hell does that look like?
- She noticed that the poll only added up to 66% way too quickly.
- Me not noticing that the poll didn't add up to 100% might explain why the bookstore isn't making enough money.
- Who are Bill Hicks and Attell?

NOVEMBER 20
2:20 PM

Comments made to Kimberly today

"Stop suggesting Bibles to the customers."

"Sharon's sweaters are fine."

"You can go home early."

NOVEMBER 20
5:40 PM

Facts about Jesus that I told Kimberly to annoy her
1. Jesus was Jewish.
2. Jesus was a socialist.
3. Jesus was a refugee.
4. Jesus was anti–death penalty.
5. Jesus was anti–school prayer (Matthew 6:5).
6. Jesus was opposed to the accumulation of wealth.
7. Jesus was silent on the issues of homosexuality and gay marriage.
8. Jesus was a brown-skinned Middle Easterner who wore sandals to the dinner table.
9. Jesus was a friend to prostitutes.

Dan's Laws of the Universe

Scripture is the basis of all religious belief. It is also the last thing in the world that will change a person's belief once that belief has been falsely cemented.

There is an inverse correlation between a certainty of a person's religious belief and their actual knowledge of Scripture.

NOVEMBER 20
8:10 PM

Update
- Bill Hicks is a stand-up comic. Wikipedia says his material is "steeped in dark comedy."

- Dave Attell is a stand-up comic. Wikipedia says that "Patton Oswald and Bill Burr have hailed him as the greatest off-color comedian alive."
- I know who Patton Oswald is.
- Now I know who Bill Burr is too.

Facts about my marriage

Jill is always talking about stuff that I know nothing about but wish I did.

Jill was the girl in high school who had seen every *Saturday Night Live* ever made, sewed her own jeans, and was listening to punk before anyone knew what punk was.

I feel like I've told Jill about every cool thing that I've ever done but she has barely scratched the surface with me.

I was married to Jill for almost six months before she told me that she was once a fire spinner at Burning Man, which is cooler than anything I've ever done in my entire life but was an afterthought for her.

There will always be a part of Jill's life that will remain a secret to me because you can only tell your second husband so much about your previous life with your dead husband.

Jill is cooler than I will ever be, which once thrilled me but now makes me feel so fucking insecure.

NOVEMBER 20
8:56 PM

Numbers for the day
   Customers: 5
   Books sold: 2
   Toys sold: 3
   Other items sold: 0
   Estimated profit: $52
   Estimated profit after paying Kimberly's salary: - $13

NOVEMBER 21
2:20 AM

Stupidest List Ever
   Bank
   Liquor store
   Citgo
   7-Eleven
   ATM

NOVEMBER 23
10:30 PM

Thanksgiving Observations
   1. When did canned cranberry sauce get replaced with twigs-and-berries shit?

2. Potatoes and stuffing always taste better out of a box. People are just too damn pretentious to admit it.

3. Jake prays before the meal. Earnestly. I expect him to be struck by lightning every time. I'm only a little disappointed, dear Lord, when it doesn't happen. Amen.

4. Sophia does not pray earnestly like her husband. She might be faking it completely. I think she thinks Jake is a dick when it comes to prayer.

5. Turkey is the shit. It's wasted on Thanksgiving. We shouldn't save it only for meals eaten with people we don't always like.

6. Four empty wine bottles? Plus beer bottles? Who did all the drinking?

7. How can people care so much about a football game when they hate both teams playing?

8. "We don't hate the players. We hate the laundry," is just the kind of stupid thing Jake likes to spout off as if he's saying it for the first time in the history of the world when I know damn well he's heard it a million times on TV because it's way too clever for him to come up with on his own.

9. Jake was a lot more likeable when he was a kid.

10. Someone needed to tell Jill's brother that working for your dad's company does not amount to financial wizardry or entrepreneurial achievement. It's called nepotism.

11. Apparently (or at least according to Jill) I didn't need to be that person.

12. When your wife is pissed at you for your "rude-ass remark" to her brother who she never sees but also

desperately wants to make a baby, you will have sex that night despite her anger.

13. Angry sex is not as unpleasant as you might think.

Things that Jill probably thinks I'm a dick about
Whole Foods rants
Tipping
Sneakers only
Clarence
Hatred of parades
Her brother
Not converting to Judaism (maybe)
Peter (maybe)
Jake (but maybe justifiably)

NOVEMBER 23
11:20 PM

What I don't understand about Jake
He owns a sheet-metal fabrication business, but he definitely didn't grow up wanting to work in sheet-metal fabrication.

He always liked Darth Vader more than Luke Skywalker, even before we knew Darth Vader would kill the Emperor and save the galaxy.

He really likes jazz.

He wears a necktie to holiday dinners even though no one is making him wear one.

I thought he was going to be a rebel.

He seems happy, but he's a tie-wearing conservative who works in the sheet-metal fabrication industry.

The teenage version of Jake would like this version of Jake.

Addition to Dan's Laws of the Universe

If the childhood version of yourself would hate the adulthood version of yourself, you suck at life.

NOVEMBER 24
12:05 AM

Star Wars Stuff

I tell people that I'm a Han Solo guy, but I'm actually a Luke Skywalker guy. I think Han Solo is kind of a dick.

Darth Vader killed billions of innocent people then saved his only son. This did not make him a good guy. Just a selfish practitioner of nepotism.

Chewbacca and the droids are brilliantly designed characters. They aren't reliant on aging actors, so they can appear in Star Wars movies forever.

Luke Skywalker's plan to rescue Han Solo from Jabba the Hutt was the most ill-conceived plan in the history of the galaxy. Get everyone captured (including yourself) so the job becomes exponentially more difficult?

NOVEMBER 24
12:20 AM

Jill's sentences before falling to sleep

"Happy Thanksgiving, honey."

"Sometimes it's okay to just let things be. To keep the peace. You know?"

"Tomorrow. Okay? I ate way too much."

"Jake seemed a little off today. Right?"

"I missed the canned cranberry sauce too. That nuts-and-raisins stuff was bullshit."

"Good luck tomorrow."

NOVEMBER 24
7:45 PM

Worst things about Black Friday
- Working
- Jake's not working
- It feels like no one else is working
- Stupidest customers of the year
- Kids everywhere
- Kimberly (also every other day)
- "No, we don't gift wrap."
- "No, we don't gift wrap."
- "No, we don't gift wrap."
- "No, we don't fucking gift wrap." (in my head)
- Not thinking of offering free gift wrapping.

Best things about Black Friday
- Most money made since I bought the store
- It ended

Other worst things about Black Friday
- Sales down 30% from last year's Black Friday
- Steve caught an old lady trying to steal half a dozen magazines and had to call the police
- I hid in the office while Steve handled the whole incident

NOVEMBER 25
11:25 PM

Revised List of Ways to Keep Jill from Getting Pregnant
1. Fake orgasms
2. Blow jobs only
3.

Number of actual beginning-to-end blow jobs I have received in two years of marriage
  0

NOVEMBER 26
9:25 AM

How I ended up at Gillette Stadium
1. Jake's buddy Shep had an extra ticket.
2. The Patriots are "only playing Miami." (no idea what this means)

3. Steve and Sharon agreed to cover the store.
4. Mom made it seem like a big deal to spend the day with Jake and his friends.
5. "Tony wanted nothing to do with this game." (no idea what this means either)

Tailgate attendees

Jake
Shep
Teja brothers (2)
Eddie the Norwegian (can't tell if he's really from Norway or if they're just fucking with me)

NOVEMBER 26
10:55 AM

This guy named Shep

Works for a Medicare advocacy organization
Does not strike me as the nonprofit type
Cousin-in-law of Tony (who wanted nothing to do with this game)
Drunk within an hour of arrival
Likes to verbally abuse strangers twice his size in Miami football jerseys
Makes a damn good twice-baked potato
"You don't like football? Why are you here?"
Made a reference to Sisyphus that I think only I understood
"At least you drink beer. Can't say the same for Matty."

Brought salad
Doesn't look like the salad type
"Why are you always writing shit down?"
I think he's a libertarian socialist, which shouldn't be a
    thing.
A really likeable asshole

NOVEMBER 26
11:45 AM

Why I'm always writing shit down
"I want to write a novel someday."
"It's all grist for the mill."
"My memory is shit."

Real reasons for lists
Compromise at first with therapist because journaling
    sucks
Finished with therapist but lists became a habit
Thinking on the page
Makes sense of things
Putting things in lists puts them out of my head and lets
    me sleep

Addition to Dan's Laws of the Universe
A habit is just an obsession that pretends to be intentional
    and controllable.

NOVEMBER 26
4:45 PM

Things I don't understand about football
1. "This is a meaningless game," but everyone wants the referee to die.
2. Why does a football fan prefer to watch the game from really far away in 14-degree temperatures with no clean bathroom for miles?
3. The tailgate food is very important, very planned, and very plentiful, but it is cooked on a grill that appears to have never been cleaned and caught fire at least once over the course of the day.
4. Not "covering the spread" (whatever that means) can make an otherwise normal man punch a plastic chair at least a dozen times.
5. Football fans will drink ice-cold beer while shivering uncontrollably.
6. Why would anyone enter a coliseum filled with drunken, mentally challenged rage-monsters wearing the colors of the opponent?
7. Why would any sane parent choose to bring a child into this environment?
8. Adult men dress up in beads and face paint and Elvis costumes so they can be featured on the jumbo TV without any hope of compensation whatsoever.

NOVEMBER 26
6:05 PM

What I understand about football now
- 10 yards is really fucking important.
- Running forward for three or four yards before being tackled is shockingly satisfying to football fans even though it looks like absolutely nothing to me.
- Long underwear, jeans, snow pants, mittens, and cold hands make the act of urinating a serious commitment.
- There is a lot less kicking than you would think for a game called football.
- Women who attend football games must never pee.
- Planning a fast exit from the parking lot is almost as important as winning the game.
- Pass interference is the thing that provokes the greatest emotional response in a football fan.
- A touchdown for a team that you have never seen before and care nothing about in a sport you barely understand will still somehow cause you to want to leap into the arms of a stranger.
- I think I would go to another football game if I didn't have to worry about frostbite.

NOVEMBER 26
7:55 PM

Places I urinated today
McDonald's restroom on the Mass Pike
Surprisingly clean porta-john

A men's room in Gillette Stadium
Behind a tree on the edge of the parking lot
Impossibly rancid porta-john (but also the same porta-john
    as earlier)
McDonald's restroom in Milford, Massachusetts
Jake's backyard (it was dark) (didn't want to wake Jake Jr.)

NOVEMBER 26
10:00 PM

Phrases spoken today that seemed to carry so much meaning
for Jake and his friends but meant nothing to me
    "Nothing was ever as good as Jags parking."
    "Corn bread in a parking lot."
    "Whiskey and a *Playboy*."
    "Tom-Fucking-Swale."

Addition to Dan's Laws of the Universe
    Just a little bit of shared language and culture can make a
        person feel like he's standing far outside of a group,
        wishing to find a way in.

Jake
    Did not adequately prepare me for the cold
    Swears more at a football game than anywhere else
    Tried to prevent me from sounding stupid about football
    I like his friends a lot.
    I can't believe he does this all the time.
    He seems so happy and relaxed. They all do. Not a worry in
        the world.
    Compared to Jake's friends, I have no real friends.

People I was slightly jealous of today
    Tony

Questions
    When did I miss out on friends like this?
    Does Jake know that I don't have any real friends? Does
       Mom? Is that why I was here today?
    What is the thing in my life that would bring my theoreti-
       cal friends together if not football?
    Would friends make things easier?

NOVEMBER 27
11:15 AM

Original list of possible names for bookstore
    Stuff Made Up in People's Heads
    Stuff People Made Up in Their Heads
    Books
    Dan's Pipe Dream
    Shut Up and Read
    Only Dan's Favorite Books (Mostly)
    Jill's Albatross
    No Benefits. Just Books.
    A New Chapter
    Books Are Better Than Sex

NOVEMBER 28
7:00 AM

Pros of Having a Baby
1. Won't stay a baby forever
2. Making it
3.

Bullshit Pros of Having a Baby
1. Someone to take care of me in old age
2. Carry on the family name

Cons of Having a Baby
1. Costs a fucking fortune
2. Repeat #1 forever
3. Dealing with shit and piss that isn't yours
4. Eats things that aren't food
5. Breastfeeding (when do I get Jill's boobs back?)
6. Baby boys pee on you
7. Gates and car seats and those goddamn cabinet locks
8. Restaurants ruined forever
9. They could potentially grow up to become assholes and/
   or freeloaders

Things I'm Willing to Do to Avoid Having a Baby
1. Hire someone to wipe my ass in old age
2. Allow the family name to disappear forever

NOVEMBER 29
10:40 AM

Reasons why I won't convert to Judaism
1. You can't just declare yourself Jewish. It's "a process."
2. Required circumcision (I'm already circumcised, but I'm standing on principle)
3. Only one fun holiday (Hanukkah)
4. Can't decide on the spelling of their one fun holiday (Hanukkah, Chanukah, Hanukah)
5. No decorations. Seriously. NONE.
6. The food is just not as good as advertised. Noodle pudding? Gefilte fish? Matzo ball soup is a ball of matzo in chicken broth. These are not good foods.
7. No anthropomorphized and/or magical creatures
8. Yarmulkes
9. Jill didn't ask me to convert
10. I don't believe in God (anymore) (I think)

Addition to Dan's Laws of the Universe
Anything that is a "process" inevitably sucks.
You can determine the objective tastiness of a food by the probability of its presence on a restaurant menu. Kugel cannot be found on your average restaurant menu, therefore it objectively sucks.

NOVEMBER 30
5:15 PM

Things I want to do before I die that can also earn me money
1. Win a sports-related bet against Jake

2. Play poker professionally
3. Perpetrate a Nigerian prince-like scam on someone (or Jake) (or Jill's brother)

NOVEMBER 30
9:39 PM

Number of times we had sex in November:
   12

Number of times I faked the orgasm:
   0

Difficulty in faking an orgasm midstream (mid-stream?)
   Incalculable

NOVEMBER 30
11:15 PM

Gift ideas for Mom
   1.
   2.

Number of days until Mom's birthday
   15

Importance of purchasing a thoughtful gift for Mom's birthday
   Considerable

Importance of remembering a gift for Mom's birthday
   Incalculable

DECEMBER

Finances
  Savings: 8,003

Income
  What I tell Jill: 1,800
  Reality: 1,275
  Jill: 2,900

Expenses
  Mortgage: 2,206
  Toyota: 276
  Honda: 318
  Car insurance: 175
  Student loans: 395
  Cable and Internet: 215
  Electric: 96
  Oil: 0
  Phones: 180
  Gas: 135
  Christmas gifts: 500+
  Christmas tree: 45
  Outside lights: 65

Brake job: 345
Other stuff: Still too much

Revised List of Financial Solutions

SHORT-TERM

Second job
Day-trading
Online poker
Write to ~~millionaires~~ billionaires

LONG-TERM

Write a novel
Thank-you note idea

UNREALISTIC BUT STILL VIABLE

Lottery

DECEMBER 2
1:30 PM

Deals We Made About Kids
1. No kids for first two years of marriage
2. One child minimum
3. Second child only if we both agree
4. No guilt allowed in second-child decision

5. 12–24-month maternity leave
6. 100% agreement required for first name
7. Full guilt-free veto on any former asshole student names
8. Dan gets choice of middle name
9. Kid gets guilt-free choice of religion post–bar/bat mitzvah

DECEMBER 3
3:50 AM

Revised but STILL Stupidest List Ever Written
    Bank or credit union
    Citgo
    7-Eleven
    ATM

LESS STUPID (but still incredibly stupid) LIST
    Fast food
    Mortenson's or Shady Glen (cash-only businesses)
    ATM
    Maybe Citgo

DECEMBER 4
9:10 AM

A New Chapter Picks of the Month for December
    Girlchild by Tupelo Hassan (redacted sections are both ingenious and lazy)

Geek Love by Katherine Dunn

The Revenge of the Radioactive Lady by Elizabeth Stuckey-
French (amazing title)

The Boy Scout Handbook (should be read by every child)
(especially basic hatchet safety section)

DECEMBER 4
12:00 PM

Stupidest questions asked this month

1. I know that the Hunger Games is a trilogy, but do you think he'll write another book?
2. How do bookstores make money if you never sell books?
3. Why don't you have a Starbucks in here like Barnes & Noble?
4. Can you help me download this book onto my iPad?
5. Could you get Stephen King or maybe Hillary Clinton to do a talk?

Number of books sold today that I love

4

Number of books sold today that I despise

19

Number of these books sold today that I despise that include vampires

6

DECEMBER 5
10:10 AM

Number of people in our home
   2

Number of hampers in our home
   9

Number of empty hampers
   0

Average length of time Jill's clean clothing remains folded in a hamper
   8 months (approximate)

Maximum time Jill's clothing has remained in a hamper
   2 years and counting (no joke)

DECEMBER 5
4:00 PM

Reasons Amy quit
   "I'm looking for a new challenge."
   "I'm hoping to become more entrepreneurial."

Real reason Amy quit
   Hated Kimberly

Remaining employees
   Steve
   Kimberly
   Jenny
   Sharon: weekends only now

DECEMBER 6
10:22 AM

Reasons I Fell in Love with Jill
   Willing to eat ice cream for breakfast, lunch, or dinner
   Might love books even more than me
   Defends the Oxford comma with passion bordering on
      fanaticism
   Best teacher I've ever known
   Love bites on my neck and ankles
   Blindly accepts me for exactly who I am
   Refuses to conform to family traditions
   Dimples
   Never sick
   Skinny-dipping
   Changes the sheets every week
   Ignores NO RIGHT ON RED signs
   Sex (even without the blow jobs)
   Hates Virginia Woolf and José Saramago
   Loves Douglas Adams and Neil Gaiman
   Little green skirt
   The way she dances
   Toes

Loves/despises Jake
Pound cake
Cries when she sees roadkill
Can drink me under the table

Reasons I Wouldn't Have Married Jill If I Hadn't Fallen in Love with Her
Wants kids
Puts things in piles
Drives a stick shift
Hampers
Clarence
Clarence drool
Clarence staring at us while we're having sex
Clarence barking at every fucking mammal smaller than him
Leaves dirty dishes in sink overnight (fucking savage)
Widow

DECEMBER 7
7:40 AM

Things I can't do
Change my oil
Accept my mortality
Abide earnestness
Eat ice cream slowly
Respect success when it began with privilege
Parallel park
Treat the tardy well

Play the ukulele
Haggle for a better price
Pretend to like a book for the sake of a sale
A pull-up

Reasons I can't play the ukulele
I haven't removed my ukulele from its case

DECEMBER 7
8:05 AM

Why this is all Mr. Sullivan's fault
Never gave up on me
Taught me to read (finally)
Started my love affair with books
Made teaching look easy
Inspired me to change lives for the better
Never told me how challenging teaching would be

The luckiest people
People who were born wanting to be bankers, lawyers,
actuaries, and surgeons
Children
Peter Pan

DECEMBER 7
8:45 AM

Days that Will Live in Infamy
December 25, 1991: Pinkie toe

May 20, 2002: Graduation without Dad
October 31, 2005: Meg leaves me
March 1, 2010: Peter
June 22, 2015: Resign teaching position

DECEMBER 7
11:55 AM

Regrets

Not going for that possible threesome with the two girls in
that limousine when I was 19
Never calling Dad
Quitting teaching
Bringing silk flowers to Laura when I was 17 years old
Hiring Kimberly
Wearing that *Melrose Place* T-shirt on New Year's Eve
Forgiving Jake for chopping off my pinkie toe
Not sticking my pinkie toe in the freezer

Mom's regret (I assume)

Giving Jake a hatchet for Christmas. Fucking Boy Scouts.

Addition to Dan's Laws of the Universe

Silk flowers, it turns out, are super practical but not as spon-
taneous as fresh cut flowers.

Laura Green's Law of the Universe

"Any gift that requires dusting does not qualify as sponta-
neous."

DECEMBER 7
1:08 PM

The *Guardian*'s "Top five regrets of the dying"
1. I wish I'd had the courage to live a life true to myself, not the life others expected of me.
2. I wish I hadn't worked so hard.
3. I wish I'd had the courage to express my feelings.
4. I wish I had stayed in touch with my friends.
5. I wish that I had let myself be happier.

Good news
    I don't have enough customers to worry about regret #2.
    My lack of friends keeps me from worries about staying in touch.
    I'm not stopping myself from being happier. It's my checking account that's keeping me from being happy.

Bad news
    None of the above is actually good news.

DECEMBER 9
7:20 AM

The *Guardian*'s list of potential stroke triggers
1. Coffee consumption (10.6%)
2. Vigorous physical exercise (7.9%)
3. Nose blowing (5.4%)
4. Sexual intercourse (4.3%)

5. Straining to defecate (3.6%)
6. Cola consumption (3.5%)
7. Being startled (2.7%)
8. Being angry (1.3%)

Number of potential stroke triggers that I have engaged in this week
    7

Probability that sexual intercourse being a stroke trigger might postpone baby making with Jill
    0%

Probability that vigorous physical activity being a stroke trigger might postpone me joining a gym
    100%

DECEMBER 9
11:45 AM

Steps required to chop off your pinkie toe
    1. Shearling-lined slippers
    2. Brand-new hatchet
    3. Fuckface brother
    4. "Ax throwing is a thing!"
    5. Gullibility
    6. Shitty aim
    7. "Don't tell Mom!"

DECEMBER 10
5:30 AM

Gift ideas for Mom
1. Flowers
2. Chocolate
3. *The Complete Idiots Guide to Dealing with In-Laws* (really exists)
4.

Only gifts Mom really wants
1. Attention
2. Validation
3. More grandchildren
4. Me to be more like Jake

Number of days until Mom's birthday:
5

Probability that Jake has already bought Mom the perfect gift
100%

DECEMBER 10
7:10 AM

Advantages to not speaking to Dad
1. No birthday present angst
2.

DECEMBER 10
7:15 AM

If I could say anything to Dad
1. I'm sorry that Mom cheated on you.
2. Yes, I know she cheated on you. I've always known.
3. I didn't cheat on you.

DECEMBER 11
4:15 PM

Additions to Dan's Laws of the Universe
1. There is an inverse relationship between the amount of money in my bank account and my weight.
2. Stupid customer questions always come in either threes or hundreds.
3. Regardless of how much time a woman has to get ready for a night out, she will always use all that time plus 15 minutes.
4. Men wearing ties buy fewer books.
5. A person's memory of the children's picture books from their youth never matches the quality of those books.
6. Customers don't like paying full price for slender novels but don't want to read long ones, either.
7. The ratio of bad mail to good mail is 500:1.
8. Yes, airline seats recline, but they do so only as a means of identifying assholes on your flight.
9. Daylight savings time should happen at noon, when it can be appreciated.

DECEMBER 12
8:20 AM

Billionaires
    Bill Gates (Melinda Gates?)
    Warren Buffet
    Larry Ellison
    Mark Cuban
    Jeff Bezos (he already has lots of my money)
    Larry Page and Sergey Brin (package deal?)
    The Koch Brothers (I'd rather go broke first)

Top 10 highest paid athletes
    Cristiano Ronaldo
    Lionel Messi
    LeBron James
    Roger Federer
    Kevin Durant
    Novak Djokovic
    Cam Newton
    Phil Mickelson
    Jordan Spieth
    Kobe Bryant

Number of athletes on this list whose names I recognize
    2

DECEMBER 13
11:45 AM

Musicians who left their bands and went on to have successful
solo careers
>Not Steve Perry

Addition to Dan's Laws of the Universe
>Journey fans who argue that Journey isn't Journey without
>Steve Perry are just whiners in need of a time machine.

DECEMBER 14
4:30 AM

Days I Live with Peter
>September 21: Wedding anniversary
>December 24: Birthday
>March 1: Death
>February 14: Letters

Days I Really Live with Peter
>Every day

Things I Like About Peter
>Shorter than me
>Hemingway fan
>Rescued Jill from boating accident (but she probably
>>wouldn't have drowned)
>Couldn't get Jill pregnant

Prematurely balding (or balded?) (past tense?)
Dead (no offense)

Things I Don't Like About Peter
Marathon runner
James Joyce fan
Good cook
Never ran out of money
December 24 birthday kind of fucks up Christmas Eve
Still exists even though he's dead
February 14 letters

DECEMBER 15
11:55 PM

Gifts purchased for Mom's birthday
Quiet by Susan Cain (passive-aggressive)
Autumnal wreath (Jill's idea)
Framed copy of her last 3 letters to the editor (BEST GIFT
    IDEA EVER)

Subjects of Mom's last 3 letters to the editor
1. The decline of Western civilization as evidenced by
   the number of baseball caps being worn by men in restaurants
2. Where has the motorcycle sidecar gone?
3. The importance of supporting street artists

Mom's responses to the framed letters to the editor
- "What is this? No. Is it . . . ? Oh my goodness."
- "This must've been Jill's idea. Right?"
- "I may switch the frames for something more stylish."
- "Are you sure this wasn't your idea, Jill?"
- "That motorcycle sidecar story may seem trivial, but I received a lot of correspondence in response to it. People have a real love affair with sidecars."
- "This is a beautiful gift, Daniel. Truly."

Jake's gift for Mom
Cooking lesson in the home of a Peruvian immigrant

Mom's response to Jake's gift
- "This is so creative, Jake."
- "She's legal. Right?"
- "Brooklyn? Brooklyn, New York?"
- "I love a good cooking class."
- "Why Peru?"
- "Are there even any good Peruvian restaurants?"
- "She doesn't smoke. Does she?"

Number of times in my life when my gift was better than Jake's gift until now
0

Addition to the LESS STUPID (but still incredibly stupid) LIST
Carnivals (no security cameras, cash only)

DECEMBER 20
6:40 AM

Memorable Christmases

Circa 1978 (age 5): Christmas breakfast at Grandpa's house. Fruit cocktail from a can. Snowball fight with Uncle Brian. Great-Grandpa's jokes. Mom and Dad squished into a recliner together.

1982: Dad comes to house for 30 minutes on Christmas morning for breakfast. Gives me a Star Wars droid factory and a yo-yo. Hugs me hard. Doesn't stay for breakfast. I don't notice him leave. No goodbye. Don't realize this until 20 years later.

1986 (age 13): Jake and I sneak downstairs in the middle of the night. Open and rewrap gifts. Jake admits to it the next day. Little bitch.

1992 (age 19): Watch *Unforgiven* in an empty movie theater. I tell Mom and Jake that I spend the day with friends.

1992 (age 20): Christmas weekend with Christine Neelon's family in Vermont. Lots of sex in basement. Vodka martinis. Creamsicles. A dog named Pathos.

2002: Volunteer at Berlin VFW. Meet Meg in kitchen while doing dishes.

2004: Christmas at Meg's parents' house. They make us sleep in separate bedrooms. We have retaliatory sex at every chance we get. My best Christmas since childhood when Mom and Dad were still together.

2005 (age 32): First Christmas after Meg leaves me. I throw the engagement ring off the Flower Bridge into Farmington River. I regret it before it even hits the water. So stupid.

2007: First Christmas with Jill on Robin Road. Her first real Christmas tree. First stringing of popcorn and cranberries. First midnight Mass. Unknowingly gave each other the same book of Billy Collins's poetry (*Taking Off Emily Dickinson's Clothes*).

2008 (age 35): Jill tells me that Peter's birthday was on Christmas Eve. She tells me this *on Christmas Eve*. I act like a dick about it. We skip midnight Mass and go to bed angry.

Addition to Dan's Laws of the Universe
Retaliatory sex is even better than make-up sex.

DECEMBER 20
7:00 AM

The December 24, 2008, argument as I remember it
   Christmas tree alight
   Pile of wrapped presents under the tree
   Fire crackling in the fireplace
   Holiday music
   Brandy cider
   "Hey, did I ever tell you . . . ?"

My completely rational and appropriate responses to this poorly timed news
   "Seriously?"

"Are you kidding me?"

"Fuck."

"I know it's Christmas Eve! That's why I'm so upset!"

"You thought that this was the right time to mention his
birthday? Right now? Tonight? Instead of say . . . April?
Or never?"

"No. I refuse to listen to little children sing Christmas
carols under stained glass with this in my head."

"Yes, I love it, but we don't get to have pretty things tonight! You fucked that up with your bullshit news."

Admitted flaw to my memory

That apartment didn't have a fireplace.

Stupid things that should only be done on television because in
real life there are no commercial breaks. Just subsequent awk-
wardness, feelings of inadequacy, and grudging apologies

1. Storming off
2. Brooding
3. Hanging up on someone
4. Slamming doors in anger
5. Throwing anything in anger
6. Turning out the light and pretending to be asleep in
   order to demonstrate your anger

Subjects that should be broached during the first three months
of dating

1. Previous marriages
2. Crazy ex-boyfriends/girlfriends
3. Allergies

4. Arrest record
5. Parents' worst attributes
6. Possible future children
7. Major surgeries
8. Religion
9. Bizarre love of Barry Manilow and Air Supply
10. Possible future vegetarianism/veganism
11. Pets
12. Past sexual encounters involving more than one person
13. Possible deal breakers (skydiving, ferrets)
14. Can you drive a stick?
15. Voting record
16. Current drug use (if any)
17. Favorite books/authors
18. Dead husband's birthday IF THAT BIRTHDAY ALSO LANDS ON A MAJOR HOLIDAY

DECEMBER 20
7:40 AM

Christmas 2008 Lessons Learned

An excellent way to ruin Christmas morning is to fight with your spouse the night before and go to bed very angry.

Jealousy of a dead man is ugly, stupid, real, and best kept hidden, particularly on the holidays.

"Your timing sucked" is never a winnable argument.

Avoiding midnight Mass does not balance the grief of a full-blown argument, but it doesn't hurt.

Additional Christmas Lessons Learned
1. *Unforgiven* is not a Christmas movie.
2. Accomplices can never be trusted.
3. Never make decisions involving $8,000 pieces of jewelry when you're emotionally charged.
4. Eating half a dozen Creamsicles in a single sitting can result in explosive diarrhea.

DECEMBER 22
6:14 PM

Things I Wish I Had Known 20 Years Ago When I Was 20
1. Every pound you add to your body will be ten times more difficult to remove.
2. Peppermint schnapps is not an acceptable substitute for mouthwash.
3. Some bras unsnap in the front.
4. Hard rolls are not hard.
5. When the opportunity for a threesome arises, take it. *Please.* It may only happen once.
6. Audiobooks are not for morons who can't read.
7. Hours spent shoveling quarters into video games in arcades will always feel like time well spent. Hours spent playing video games at home will not.
8. You need not camouflage your condom purchases with bottles of shampoo, boxes of cookies, and ballpoint pens. No one fucking cares about your sex life.
9. Tighten lug nuts using an actual tire iron. Fingers alone won't do it.

10. Garbage disposals are not equipped to handle one pound of overcooked linguini.
11. Your hair will never be as important as you think it is until it starts falling out.
12. There is no good reason to ever set foot inside a strip club.
13. Invest in an index fund. Compound interest is so fucking important.

Things I Still Need to Do

Invest in an index fund. Compound interest is so fucking important.

DECEMBER 23
9:25 AM

Mistakes I made with Meg

1. Asked her to marry me
2. Thought that long-term financial security was at least as important as love
3. Assumed that a fiancée who is still having sex with you still loves you and isn't as unhappy as she seems to me.

DECEMBER 24
7:50 AM

15 Truths about Peter

1. He would've been 38 years old today.
2. It's a terrible thing to know that you found love only because another man died.

3. Peter had no middle name because his mother and father couldn't agree on one.
4. Peter and I would never have been friends.
5. Peter was left-handed.
6. I never met Peter, but I feel like he is always with me.
7. Peter loved Three Stooges movies, which seems ultra-cool until you watch those stupid movies and realize how stupid they are.
8. There are three photos of Peter and Jill in our house.
9. It is impossible to compete with a dead man.
10. Jill doesn't talk about Peter very often because of me.
11. Sometimes I whisper, "Thank you, Peter." Not for dying but for being so good to Jill when he was alive.
12. I suck when it comes to Peter.
13. I sometimes wonder if I think about Peter more than Jill does.
14. I will never be as good a man as Peter was.
15. Happy birthday, Peter.

DECEMBER 25
12:55 PM

Christmas presents from Mom to me
   Good to Great by Jim Collins ("For your business!")
   Gift certificate to Tracy and Company (her favorite hair salon)
   Three-month gym membership

Christmas presents from Mom to Jake
    Season pass to the Playhouse on Park
    Slippers
    Peanut brittle

Christmas presents from me and Jill to Jake Jr.
    A Wrinkle in Time series
    10 packs of Magic: The Gathering cards
    4 movie passes

Christmas presents from me to Jake Jr. that Jill didn't know about
    Nerf rifle

DECEMBER 25
1:10 PM

Number of times Mom mentioned Peter (*a man she never met*) on Christmas
    2 (way too many)

Number of books Mom gave to a son *who owns a bookstore*
    1 (also way too many)

Number of times Mom mentioned Jake and Sophia's "new downtown location"
    Lost count

Mom's mentions of Peter
"Do you still talk to Peter's mother?"
(looking at a photo of Peter and Jill) "I wish I had a chance
to meet Peter. He looks smart."

Addition to Dan's Laws of the Universe
"Looking smart" is not a thing.

DECEMBER 25
6:00 PM

Christmas Day arguments between Jake and me
The Scooby-Doo Mystery Machine shouldn't have the
name THE MYSTERY MACHINE written on the side because
the gang stumbles upon mysteries. They don't seek them out.

Chilean sea bass is actually Patagonian toothfish, and that is
what we should call it. Fuck the pretentious renaming of food.

"Scantily clad" is a stupid way of describing someone.

The word "porn" makes pornography dirtier than it really is.

DECEMBER 25
6:10 PM

5 reasons to never use the phrase "scantily clad" again
1. "Scantily clad" has been done. It's been overdone. It's
    absolutely, positively finished. Beaten like a dead horse.
    It's moved past cliché and into the realm of tragically

unoriginal. It's a phrase that you should never, ever use again.

2. It's weird that the word "scantily" is never used without the word "clad."

3. It's weird that the phrase is almost exclusively used to describe a woman in a certain state of undress when men are just as capable of being in similar states of undress.

4. The phrase "scantily clad" is also a little creepy. Not a lot creepy. Just a teensy-weensy bit creepy. It's the kind of phrase that mouth-breathing teenage fantasy writers use to describe the inexplicably half-naked girl being held prisoner by the dragon, and that makes it a tiny bit creepy.

5. Do a Google image search of the phrase "scantily clad." The images associated with the phrase should make it clear that this is not a phrase that you should be using.

DECEMBER 25
6:30 PM

Other poorly named foods (in addition to Chilean sea bass)
Corned beef
Pulled pork
Bread pudding
Noodle pudding
Field greens
Blood orange
Pu pu platter

DECEMBER 25
7:00 PM

Alcohol consumed on Christmas
    Mom: 3 glasses of wine
    Jill: 2 glasses of wine, both unfinished (annoying)
    Jake: 4 glasses of wine and at least 4 beers
    Sophia: Half a bottle of champagne
    Jake Jr.: None
    Me: 2 beers

DECEMBER 25
10:55 PM

Things I Learned on Christmas Day
- Being sober sucks when your mother and brother are not.
- Sophia goes ice fishing on her own and loves it.
- There are FIVE books in the *Wrinkle in Time* series now.
- Jake and Sophia's new location is "booming."
- Goldfish were originally treated like fresh flowers. Colorful decorations for a room that were never fed and simply discarded when they died.
- I am the only person in my family who thinks that *Die Hard* is a Christmas movie.
- The Gambia is the name of a country that runs along the Gambia River. It's called *The* Gambia so it won't be confused with Zambia.
- Jake Jr. hates his name.

DECEMBER 25
11:10 PM

5 Reasons Why Jake Jr. Has Every Right to Hate His Name
1. Naming your child after yourself is self-serving and narcissistic.
2. No one likes to be called Junior. Ever.
3. Living in the permanent shadow of your father sucks.
4. Being required to write your father's name (and especially Jake's name) on tests and official documents when you're angry at your father really sucks.
5. If Jake Jr. also decides to name his son Jake, then his son becomes "the third," which makes everyone want to punch him.

DECEMBER 25
11:30 PM

Additions to Dan's Laws of the Universe
1. The number of drinking stories that a person wants to tell is in direct proportion to the amount of alcohol he or she has consumed.
2. The quality of a person's drinking stories is in inverse proportion to the amount of alcohol he or she has consumed.
3. *Die Hard* is a Christmas movie. So is *Die Hard 2*.

Addition to Dan's Laws of the Universe
Don't sleep on *Die Hard 2*. It might be an even better Christmas movie than *Die Hard*.

DECEMBER 26
10:35 AM

Dan's 6 Rules of Drinking Stories
1. No one will ever care about your drinking stories as much as you.
2. Drinking stories never impress the type of woman you want to impress.
3. If you have more than three excellent drinking stories from your entire life, you do not understand what constitutes an excellent drinking story.
4. Drinking stories must always be your own. No one cares about what your buddy did when he was drunk.
5. Even the best drinking stories are seriously compromised if told during the daytime and/or at the workplace.
6. Old people's drinking stories are acceptable in any form, as they are rare and oftentimes hilarious.

DECEMBER 27
6:14 PM

Problems with Clarence
Takes my spot on the couch
Labradoodle is an embarrassing name for a breed of dog
Clarence is an embarrassing name for a dog
Life expectancy: 12–14 years
Only nine years old
Peter's dog

DECEMBER 28
8:30 AM

Shopping List
  Dog food
  Stamps
  Miracle Whip
  Diet A&W root beer
  Two ripe avocados
  Baking soda
  Little Debbie Snack Cakes
  Powerball ticket

Additions to Dan's Laws of the Universe
  There is nothing miraculous about Miracle Whip. It's just
    mayonnaise, which means it's fucking disgusting.
  Avocados are a bullshit food that are only ripe for about 14
    seconds.
  Walk around with Diet Coke and half a dozen assholes will
    tell you how bad it is for you. Walk around with diet
    root beer and no one says a word.
  No one knows what baking soda does.

DECEMBER 29
7:00 PM

Things no one warned me about when I bought the bookstore
  1. Inventory at the end of every month
  2. Cheap bastards who return travel books after their
      vacation

3. Books are heavy
4. Certain books attract asshole readers who ruin the book for me
5. So much squatting
6. Most stolen book is The Bible

DECEMBER 29
7:00 PM

Only good things about December inventory
1. Kim's birthday so Steve helped instead
2. Jill brought pizza and cookies
3. Fewer books to count with the holiday sales
4. Jill flashed me as she left to boost my spirits

Addition to Dan's Laws of the Universe
Never underestimate the power of a little public nudity.

DECEMBER 29
11:50 PM

Steve
- Former college football tight end
- Father of infant twin boys who never complains about anything and always looks happy and well rested, which makes me hate him a little
- Not much of a reader yet can sell a book to anyone

- Steve in his interview: "Business is people. Not product. A good salesman can sell anything if he likes people and money. I like both a lot."
- Carries two dollar bills in his wallet at all times
- Eats standing up
- Steve in his interview: "My father once said that you can't learn everything in a book, and you can't learn everything in a bar."
- I feel a little ridiculous being Steve's boss. He's a better human being than me in every way. He should probably just orchestrate a rebellion, depose me, and assume control of the store. I wouldn't blame him.
- I like Steve a lot.
- I wish Steve liked me.

DECEMBER 31
11:59 PM

Last 30 minutes of 2017
    NBC
    Champagne
    Dick Clark lament
    Oyster regret
    Second base
    Stick
    Pee
    Countdown
    Little pink plus

Countdown
Happy New Year
Toast to the New Year
Ginger ale

JANUARY

New Year's Resolutions
1. Don't run out of money.
2. Don't let Jill find out that we're running out of money.
3. Don't find out the sex of my unborn child.
4. Don't end up in jail.
5. Don't kill Clarence.
6. Open an index fund.
7. Increase store sales by at least 20%.
8. Find a way to increase store sales by at least 20%.
9. Three Little Debbie Snack Cakes per week <u>maximum</u>.
10. Open at least one of Dad's letters.
11. Read those other two *Wrinkle in Time* books.
12. Learn how to do baby stuff like putting on a diaper and other stuff that I don't know I don't know (there must be more stuff to learn than just diapers).
13. Build something for the baby. Anything. Learn to do something with my hands that isn't embarrassing or stupid.
14. Don't ruin my unborn child's life before he or she is born.

JANUARY 2
4:00 PM

12 things I didn't know
1. Jill is already 4 to 8 weeks pregnant. Maybe more. She says it just works that way.
2. Pregnancy is not "an emergency." We need to wait TWO WEEKS before a doctor's appointment. Grow a *brand-new person* inside your body and doctors say, "Meh."
3. Telling your wife that her pregnancy is "an emergency" does not go over well.
4. Apparently the pregnant lady hormones start early.
5. Telling your wife that the pregnant lady hormones "apparently start early" does not go over well.
6. Asking if we can still have sex five minutes after the pink plus sign does not go over well.
7. Jill has been pregnant for two days (or 4 to 8 weeks according to her) and I've already done everything wrong.
8. It's possible to fall in love with a tiny collection of cells that you've never seen before at the instant you know those cells exist.
9. Women who have never been pregnant seem to know a lot about being pregnant.
10. Words get more complicated when someone has a baby growing inside them.
11. Getting your wife pregnant does not make you feel more like a man.

12. Women sometimes poop during delivery. I did not know this. I did not want to know this. I have no idea what I am going to say if this happens, but it will most assuredly be wrong.

JANUARY 3
6:17 AM

Finances
  Savings: 6,921

Income
  What I tell Jill: 3,000
  Reality: 2,280
  Jill: 2,900

Expenses
  House: 2,206
  Toyota: 276
  Honda: 318
  Car insurance: 175
  Student loans: 395
  Cable and Internet: 215
  Electric: 112
  Oil: 612
  Phones: 180
  Gas: 120
  New purse: 212 (WTF?)

JANUARY 3
6:29 AM

Revised Financial Solutions (and potential drawbacks)

SHORT-TERM

Second job: Jill would know we're in trouble and I have no
time for a second job.
Day-trading: Requires initial investment. Might be harder
than it seems.
Online poker: See day-trading.

LONG-TERM

Write a novel: Takes a year or more to write. No guaran-
tees. And I might suck as a writer.
Thank-you note idea: No idea how to start.

UNREALISTIC BUT STILL VIABLE

Write to billionaires: Seems impossible, but it only takes
one.
Lottery: Unlikely

JANUARY 4
8:10 AM

DAYS WITHOUT

Chocolate glazed doughnuts	503
Gum	72
Crying	3 (approximately)
Little Debbie Snack Cakes	2
Green vegetables	12
Crying	3 (approximately)
Flossing	5
Retail rage	2
Regret over quitting my job	0
Dad	5,707

JANUARY 4
8:40 AM

First 5 minutes of every day
    Shut off alarm
    Climb over Clarence
    Pee
    Log on to banking app (while still on toilet)
    Hold breath
    Panic
    Cry (only sometimes)

Mayrock's Taxonomy of Crying
  Choked Up
  Lip Quiver
  Whining Moan
  Sniffling Tears
  Rivers of Tears
  Awkward Heaving
  Weeping
  Snot Bubbles

FREQUENCY OF MY CRYING

Choked Up	5%
Lip Quiver	21%
Whining Moan	35%
Sniffling Tears	25%
Rivers of Tears	12%
Awkward Heaving	0%
Weeping	1%
Snot Bubbles	1%

JANUARY 4
12:30 PM

My problems with Little Debbie Snack Cakes, broken down into
percentages
  25%: Too many calories
  10%: No nutritional value
  35%: Embarrassing name
  30%: Most irresistible food item ever

JANUARY 4
7:10 PM

Three kinds of people
1. People who make their dreams come true because they were told that it was possible
2. People who make their dreams come true because they were told that it was impossible and they are hell-bent on proving the world wrong
3. Me

JANUARY 5
5:10 PM

Physical thank-you note vs. email thank-you note flowchart
1. Is the recipient the kind of inane and pedantic person who would be offended by an email in lieu of a hand-written thank-you note?
   - If NO, send an email. Not only is it more efficient, it allows you to say more in less time.
   - If YES, answer the following:
2. Is the recipient someone whose opinions you care about?
   - If NO, send an email.
   - If YES, consider sending an email. If you're still uncertain, answer the following question.
3. Is the recipient the kind of small-minded, vacuous person who might underhandedly complain about your failure to send an actual thank-you note to people who you know and respect?

- If NO, send the email.
- If YES, grudgingly send the thank-you note. Curse it before sending if you are a voodoo priest.

4. When these rules are unavailable to you, you can always rely on this one question to arrive at an equitable solution:

   Is the recipient a backward-thinking, arcane traditionalist capable of underhanded, passive-aggressive, prickish behavior with far too much time on their hands?

   - If NO, send an email.
   - If YES, send a thank-you note. Or better yet, eradicate this person from your life entirely if possible.

JANUARY 6
7:00 AM

Number of Letters from Dad since June
6

Number of Letters I've Told Jill About
1

Number of Letters I've Opened
0

JANUARY 8
7:45 AM

LESS STUPID (but still incredibly stupid) LIST
Fast food
ATM
Maybe Citgo
Carnival

JANUARY 11
9:35 AM

A New Chapter Picks of the Month for January
Wonder by R.J. Palacio (I thought it was only good, but I'd
never admit to it)
Free-Range Chickens by Simon Rich
Holidays on Ice by David Sedaris (I've always thought of
myself as an unfunny David Sedaris)
The Tale of Despereaux by Kate DiCamillo (best children's
book ever)
Popular by Maya Van Wagenen (Jill's addition to the list)

JANUARY 11
10:35 AM

Books You Should Not Read
The Ugly Duckling (we hate you till you're beautiful)
Blindness by José Saramago (made Jill weep and his lack of
paragraphing is absurd)

The Secret by Rhonda Byrne (some secrets aren't worth
keeping)

Love You Forever by Robert Munsch (you can't un-see some
of those last pictures)

The Missing Piece by Shel Silverstein (love steals away your
identity and your song)

JANUARY 12
3:30 PM

Possible reasons why Kimberly doesn't have any gay friends
and doesn't know any gay people
- She doesn't have many friends to begin with (possible)
- She's a bigot and her gay friends know it (probable)
- She's part of a frighteningly insular community where
  gay people exist but would be ostracized or worse if
  they ever revealed themselves (likely)

JANUARY 13
10:10 AM

Things I like to imagine would be different if Dad hadn't left
1. I'd be playing in the town softball league.
2. I'd be able to hang pictures on the walls.
3. I'd be able to watch a football game and understand
   what the fuck is going on.
4. I'd drink more beer and less wine.

5. I wouldn't have run away from that fight with Jimbo Powers.
6. I'd be able to skip rocks and make armpit noises.
7. I'd like the Rolling Stones. Maybe Bob Dylan, too.
8. I'd know how to be a father.
9. I would get lost less often.
10. I wouldn't be so afraid.

JANUARY 14
12:25 PM

Books I pretend to have read
   Everything by Leo Tolstoy
   Wuthering Heights
   Atlas Shrugged
   Everything by Jonathan Franzen (except the half of *The Corrections* that I actually read)
   Comic books
   Everything by Dr. Seuss

Books I've tried to read and now only pretend to have read
   Catch-22
   The Sound and the Fury
   Moby-Dick
   How to Win Friends & Influence People

Books I wouldn't even pretend to have read if you paid me
   Anything by James Joyce
   Anything by Virginia Woolf

JANUARY 15
8:30 PM

10 Rules I Break

1. I never worry about dating a document correctly because no one cares if the document is dated correctly unless they tell you to date it correctly.

2. I make right turns on red when the coast is clear even when there is a sign indicating that it's illegal, because waiting for no conceivable reason is insanity.

3. I ignore dress codes whenever possible because the only people who really care if you are conforming to the dress code are the worst possible people (the same people who expect hand-written thank-you notes). Also, everyone is way too busy thinking that everyone is looking at them to worry about me. Also, you have a right to feel good about the way you look.

4. When I am using a single-user restroom and someone tests the doorknob, finds it locked, and then knocks, I refuse to answer, because this behavior is lunacy. Isn't a locked door signal enough that it's occupied?

5. When asked for my position on a document, I write "Upright" every time.

6. When parking my car at a gas station or rest area with the sole intent of going inside to use a restroom or make a purchase, I park in front of a gas pump as if I'm also purchasing gas if no closer space is available.

7. I eat the food in the grocery store that I plan on buying (usually candy bars, soda, Pop-Tarts, and fruit)

and then scan the bar codes on the empty wrappers at the checkout. This is occasionally a problem with food that is paid for by the pound (bananas and apples).

8. I treat red lights as stop signs after 1:00 AM.
9. I jaywalk.
10. I use single-user restrooms designated for women if the men's room is occupied and no woman is waiting.

JANUARY 16
10:30 AM

Comments from doctor during my physical

Your gown is on backward.

Your blood pressure is good.

Your blood pressure is the only good news I have for you.

You've gained 20 pounds over the past two years.

You were already 10 pounds overweight.

Your cholesterol has gone from borderline to high.

You're going to be a father. You need to start taking care of yourself.

Do you want to be the kind of guy who starts taking pills in your forties?

Yes, I know you're 37. I'm your doctor.

Turn and cough.

JANUARY 16
10:41 AM

Four comments on the gown
1. Calling it a gown is more than a little ridiculous.
2. Inventing a gown that covers your ass might make some-one a lot of money.
3. If an ass-covering gown could be invented, it would've already been invented.
4. This is probably what every failed inventor says.

JANUARY 16
10:55 AM

Fears
1. Hypodermic needles
2. Erectile dysfunction
3. Fatherhood
4. Sharks
5. The sharks I can't see
6. The possibility of sharks I can't see
7. Icicles
8. Assumed silent comparisons to Peter
9. Asparagus pee
10. Asteroids (not the video game)
11. Unleashed dogs
12. Dad walking into bookstore unannounced
13. Losing the house
14. Public speaking
15. Butt crack sweat on my pants

Addition to Dan's Laws of the Universe
Fucking *Jaws* ruined the ocean.

JANUARY 17
6:45 AM

Things we all absolutely want but for some reason can't get
1. A vacation from a vacation
2. The four-day workweek
3. The elimination of all dress codes
4. The elimination of the electoral college
5. Teleportation
6. Cellular telephone jamming technology in every movie theater
7. Decent rest areas along the Saw Mill River and Taconic Parkway
8. Five more seasons of *The Office*
9. A national holiday on the Monday following the Super Bowl

JANUARY 18
2:30 AM

Questions
1. How does someone just disappear for 15 years?
2. Did he stop loving me?
3. Has he started loving me again?
4. Why?
5. What changed?
6. Why these letters now?

JANUARY 19
10:00 AM

Important questions to ask about a religion before joining (or choosing to remain a member)

KURT METZGER'S LIST

1. How much does it cost?
2. Does God do the killing or will I be required to kill on his behalf?
3. Do I need to stay in the religion for Mom or Dad, and what penalties (if any) will I suffer if I choose to exit the religion?

MY ADDITIONS TO KURT'S LIST

1. Do women enjoy full and absolute equality within the religion?
2. Is the church open to all people, regardless of race, nationality, marital status, sexual preference, criminal history, occupation, etc.?
3. How often and how long are services?
4. Do you need to cut your penis in order to join?
5. Can you wear jeans to services?
6. Will you be passing a plate and keeping my donation between myself and God, or will you be billing me like a car dealership?

JANUARY 20
3:35 PM

Number of people with ideas on how to improve the bookstore this week
  6

Number of books actually purchased by these people
  2

Number of viable, potentially profitable ideas offered
  0

Worst idea
  "Sell pets. Market them as the kinds of pets that Harry and
  Ron and Hermione had. Owls, cats, rats, and such."

Second worst idea
  "Maybe you could rent books instead of sell them. Kind of
  like a library. Just more expensive."

Books I really should get around to reading
  The Harry Potter series

JANUARY 20
6:30 PM

Words I thought I'd never say that I said this week
  We need another *Fifty Shades* and soon.
  I should've ordered more *Vogue* and *Seventeen*.

That meter maid is just doing his job, miss.
I have a headache, honey. Can I get a rain check?

JANUARY 20
9:10 PM

The evolution of my understanding of my parents' divorce
- "Dad and I just don't love each other in that way anymore."
- "When your father lost his job, he became a different person."
- "I was feeling so alone when I met Ted."
- "No, it was at least six months between the divorce and the wedding. At least."
- "Fine. I guess it was three months."
- "I meant three months rounded up."

Why my father stopped calling or taking us on his visitations
- I think he still loved Mom and couldn't stand to see her with another man.
- I think he was ashamed of losing his wife to another man.
- I think he was ashamed of being so poor.
- Two rooms, a hot plate, and a concrete floor in the back of a liquor store is not a great place to bring your kids.
- Absence and neglect is like an index fund. It compounds over time until it is enormous and impossible to overcome.

Why my father still should've remained in our lives
- You don't get to divorce your kids just because your wife left you for another man.
- Kids don't give a shit about concrete floors and hot plates.
- When your kids don't make an effort to see you because they are kids, you should act like an adult or risk fucking them up for life.

JANUARY 21
3:25 PM

Reasons Mom wanted to have lunch
Try out the new bakery in the center
"Catch up"
"Chat"

Real reasons Mom wanted to have lunch
"You need to start dressing like a real businessman."
"You should ask Jake and Sophia for business advice."
"Maybe you should grow a goatee."
"Is Jill happy?"

Mom's latest fads
Juicing
Bingo
Mime class
Step counting

JANUARY 21
5:15 PM

Four things to know before commenting negatively on another person's choice of clothing (inspired by Kim)
1. You're an awful person for doing so. Always.
2. Be aware that you have failed to evolve beyond the mentality of your average high school bully.
3. Be apprised that you are likely suffering from poor self-esteem and a negative self-image.
4. Your comments reveal you to be a petty, small, and mean-spirited jerk-face to the rest of the world.

JANUARY 22
8:05 PM

Things I once loved but now hate
  Libraries
  Snow days
  My 2002 Subaru Baja
  Discounted hardcovers
  Amazon.com
  Clarence (I loved him for about a week)
  Valentine's Day

Things I once hated but now love
  Fifty Shades of Vampire fan fiction
  Thomas the Tank Engine toys
  Monty Python

JANUARY 23
11:25 PM

Best and worst thing to come from lunch with Mom
    Bingo

Best things about bingo
    1. Cash only
    2. Large amounts of cash (according to Mom)
    3. No security cameras (probably)
    4. Old people
    5. Slow people

Worst thing about bingo
    1. Actually possible
    2. A real solution
    3. Can't stop thinking about it

JANUARY 24
4:05 AM

Alterations on my daily routine
    No alarm (couldn't sleep)
    Climb over Clarence (still sleeping)
    Google (while on toilet)
    Don't even feel like maybe crying

JANUARY 24
4:25 AM

Bingo Halls in Connecticut
 St. Vincent De Paul, East Haven
 VFW Post 7788, Milford
 VFW Post 9929, West Hartford
 Most Holy Trinity Church Bingo, Wallingford
 American Legion, Wolcott
 Chesterfield Fire Company, Oakdale
 St. Isaac Jogues Church, East Hartford

Additions to Dan's Laws of the Universe
 The Internet makes everything easier and everyone lazier.
 The Internet makes possibly disastrous, insane decisions seem
  so much more doable.

JANUARY 24
12:45 PM

Contents of waiting room
 46 chairs
 3 coffee tables
 7 copies of January edition of *Parents* magazine
 9 copies of December edition of *Fit Pregnancy*
 2 copies of *Highlights*
 9 human beings
 At least 3 fetuses (our fetus included) (visual inspection
  only)

Addition to Dan's Laws of the Universe
>Parents say it's *their* child (or fetus), like they own it, and in some ways it's true, but not in the same way you own socks or a coffee table or even a dog. Not even close.

JANUARY 24
12:52 PM

Notes from my first *Highlights* experience
- "Bison biting burritos" is hardly a tongue twister.
- *Goofus and Gallant* demonstrates an utter lack of nuance.
- Hidden Pictures has gotten a lot harder since I was a kid.
- Part of me wants to submit a poem to "Your Own Pages" and see if it would be accepted.
- "Tootie wears a turquoise tutu" is also a shitty tongue twister.
- I strongly suspect that every "Dear Highlights" letter is fabricated bullshit.

JANUARY 24
12:54 PM

Highlights-related addendum
>It seems a little racist that the black girl from *The Facts of Life* was named Tootie.
>I wonder if the same people who write the fake *Penthouse* letters write the fake *Highlights* letters. I really, really hope so.

JANUARY 24
2:50 PM

Incredible stuff
    Heartbeat
    Vaginal ultrasound
    There are male ob-gyns

JANUARY 24
4:00 PM

New information on Jill
- Blood type O
- 126 pounds
- Inconsistent periods
- Heavy flow, little cramping
- Went on the pill when she was 16
- Went off the pill for three years while she and Peter were married
- Already taking prenatal vitamins
- Chicken pox at age 12
- Tay-Sachs screening done when married to Peter
- Does not want a C-section
- Already 11 weeks pregnant
- Due date July 20

New information about Dan
- Happy Jill's doctor is a woman
- Doesn't know what Tay-Sachs is

- Afraid to ask what Tay-Sachs is
- Afraid of Tay-Sachs but also afraid of sounding stupid
- ". . . while Peter and I were married" shouldn't bother me as much as it does

JANUARY 25
4:15 AM

Truths about Peter
- My wife wouldn't be my wife if Peter were alive.
- The tiny collection of cells that I already love would not exist if Peter were alive.
- The person who dates the girl last usually wins unless the guy before him died. Then the person who dates the girl last can never win. He's always a consolation prize.
- If Jill could change the past, she would absolutely not let Peter die, which I would understand completely, but it would also break my heart and is breaking it a little already.

JANUARY 27
6:15 PM

Pregnancy Questions
- How accurate is this supposed due date?
- Does the milk come before the baby or after the baby?
- How long into the pregnancy can Jill and I still have sex?
- Is one glass of wine really okay?

- If the baby nurses for a year, does that mean Jill's boobs are off-limits *for a year?*
- Why are car seats so fucking expensive?
- What does "water breaking" really mean?

Ways in which the previous list is like the shopping cart of a teenager purchasing condoms

Only one item is real. The rest are just camouflage to disguise the one answer I really want.

JANUARY 28
5:45 PM

Thoughts on today's fucking baptism

- When did the baptism become a complex social affair that steals my entire afternoon?
- Isn't a cake in the shape of a cross sacrilegious?
- Would it be more sacrilegious if a Jesus had been added to the cross?
- If Jesus had been added to the cross, would it be wrong to ask for "a little bit of Christ's thigh" or "a bit of his left flank"?
- Asking your wife's friend why her child's baptism isn't more accurately called a "religious indoctrination ceremony" is apparently not as clever and amusing as you might think.
- I'm not allowed to say "indoctrination" at a baptism, but it's apparently perfectly okay to say "fucking asshole" and "Fuck off, Dan."

- Telling your wife that she doesn't understand your position on baptismal indoctrination because she is a Jew is not a good idea.
- If our baby is a boy and we have a bris, can I order a penis cake?
- Asking your wife about a penis cake at the baptism is also not a good idea.
- Asking your wife about a penis cake at any time is probably not a good idea.
- Insisting that you are serious about a penis cake (because you are) is not a good idea.
- Theme cakes are stupid reminders of why we're here.
- Religious rituals for babies include "dunk the baby" or "cut the penis."
- It sucks to be a baby.

JANUARY 28
7:40 PM

Regrets

1. Not including "circumcision at the hospital" in our baby negotiations.
2. I didn't read Bill Cosby's *Fatherhood* before I discovered he was a sex offender and now I can't read it even though I heard it was great.
3. I didn't watch House of Cards before I discovered that Kevin Spacey was gross, so now I can't watch it even though I heard it was very good but not great.

JANUARY 29
1:45 PM

Goals

1. Locate cash
2. Determine amount of cash
3. Identify entrances and exits
4. Identify possible escape routes
5. Identify possible threats
6. Don't be memorable

"A human being should be able to" (according to science-fiction writer Robert Heinlein)

Change a diaper (no)

Plan an invasion (not unless I'm playing Risk)

Butcher a hog (no)

Conn a ship (what does this mean?)

Design a building (no)

Write a sonnet (not a good one)

Balance accounts (yes, but Excel spreadsheets are confusing as fuck)

Build a wall (LEGO)

Set a bone (no)

Comfort the dying (doubtful)

Take orders (absolutely)

Give orders (unfortunately no)

Cooperate (sometimes)

Act alone (yes)

Solve equations (depends because $1+1=2$ is an equation)

Analyze a new problem (yes, but the quality of the analysis is not guaranteed)

Pitch manure (where?)

Program a computer (no)

Cook a tasty meal (theoretically)

Fight efficiently (depends on the size of the opponent)

Die gallantly (highly unlikely)

JANUARY 29
11:40 PM

Notes from VFW #9929 (South Street, West Hartford, Connecticut)

1. Secondhand smoke. Holy shit. Was it really this bad 20 years ago?
2. No visible weapons (except for the enormous artillery piece on front lawn)
3. Three doors—all unlocked, including rear door to kitchen (smell = ew)
4. 200+ players
   a. All men
   b. Average age: 75 (no exaggeration)
   c. Number of players under 50 years old: > 10
   d. Number of players under 40 years old: 0
5. $100 buy-in—all cash—$20K total pot
6. Cash at the bar, too. How much? Worth the additional risk?
7. Sticky floor. Gross. Impede escape?
8. I was leaving when Bill stopped me.
9. Bingo is an incredibly stupid game.

Bill Donovan

"Hey, you. I haven't seen you here before."

72 years old

Vietnam veteran

Biceps

Harbormaster turned MP

Corporal

"Who the fuck is Klinger?"

"You going to play or what?"

Slight limp

"You either hate the new guy because he's an unknown, or you love the new guy because he's an unknown. I usually like the new guy. Unless he's an asshole."

Widower

"Don't ask me questions about my wife. I said she died. All you need to know is she's dead."

"Yes, of course bingo sucks."

"These guys are too old or two stupid to play Hold'em."

The only time he took fire in Vietnam was when an MP on base mistook him for the enemy.

"I was drafted, dummy. Do I look like a fucking hero to you?"

"The whole damn country was FUBAR. Every inch of that place was FUBAR."

Four beers in less than an hour

"Why you taking notes? This isn't a skill game. It's just blind luck."

"You don't follow any sports? Nothing? Not even baseball?"

Googled
MP = military police
FUBAR = Fucked up beyond all recognition
Hold'em = Texas Hold'em (poker)

QUESTIONS

1. Is there a less male-dominated, less militarily inclined bingo night? Old lady night? Preschool night? Disability night?
2. Is the money centrally located at any one point?
3. Why do people play this fucking game? It's like the lottery plus ink and effort.
4. How much does $20K weigh? How much space does it take up?
5. Why does every man in a VFW look so angry?

New Problems:
1. Getaway vehicle?
    - Can't use mine
    - Can't rent

- Can't borrow
- Can't steal (don't know how)
2. Alibi?
   - Why do I need one?
   - Maybe I don't need one.
   - How is an alibi even possible if you can't be in two places at the same time?
   - Only suspects need an alibi.
   - If I'm a suspect, it's all over.

Reasons why it's "all over" if police declare me a suspect
1. I can't lie.
2. I'm afraid of the police.
3. I'm a conflict-averse people-pleaser.
4. I crack while trying to enforce the bookstore's more-than-reasonable return policy.

What will this make me?
- Thief?
- Robber?
- ~~Burglar?~~
- Plunderer?
- Bandit?
- ~~Pirate?~~ (I wish)
- Criminal?
- ~~Robin Hood?~~
- Hero?

JANUARY 30
2:05 AM

New Thought
>I need a theme song for this. First lyric that came to mind:
>*I fought the law, and the law won.*

Amount of time it took for me to realize the implications of this lyric
>Way too fucking long

Possible theme songs
- "Stayin' Alive": Disco sucks unless Jill is dancing to it
- "Bingo": Obvious, uninspiring, and just the kind of uncool thing I would do
- "Mo Money Mo Problems": BS sung by someone who isn't staring at the possibility of admitting to his pregnant wife that he's a failure and they're going to lose the house
- "Take the Money and Run": My name isn't Billy Joe or Bobbie Sue
- "Money for Nothing" by Dire Straits: Too cool for me
- "Money, Money, Money" by ABBA: The perfect song for me, but I would never admit to it

Probability that I'm trying to find a theme song to avoid the reality of this plan
>High

JANUARY 31
7:18 AM

Thing I realized about myself today
I'm a conflict-averse people-pleaser

Thing I hate most about myself
I'm a conflict-averse people-pleaser

FEBRUARY

FEBRUARY 1
7:12 AM

Finances
    Savings: 4,603

Income
    What I tell Jill: 2,300
    Reality: 1,033
    Jill: 2,900

Expenses
    House: 2,206
    Toyota: 276
    Honda: 318
    Car insurance: 175
    Student loans: 395
    Cable and Internet: 215
    Electric: 132
    Oil: 446
    Phones: 180
    Gas: 101

Financial Solutions

FRONT BURNER

- Bingo
- Begging billionaires
- "No Thank-You Note Required" greeting card

BACK BURNER

- Second job
- Day-trading

Bingo To-Do List
1. Identify best possible bingo locations
2. Figure out what else needs to be added to this list

Begging Billionaire To-Do List
1. Write letter
2. Find addresses
3. Send letters
4. Wait

"No Thank-You Note Required" To-Do List
1. Design a prototype
2. Find a partner maybe?
3. Tell Jill maybe?
4. Learn how to manufacture and sell shit

Why thank-you notes (in response to gifts) are stupid

1. Only uppity, pretentious assholes with enormous amounts of discretionary time value the receipt of a thank-you note.

2. Most thank-you notes contain trite, repetitive, meaningless bits of mundanity.

3. Expecting a thank-you note in exchange for your gift turns the act of giving into an asymmetrical trade: I give you a gift in exchange for a bit of card stock, an inconsequential amount of ink, an envelope, and possibly a stamp.

4. The expectation of a thank-you note turns an act of generosity into a bullshit etiquette trap.

Why my "No Thank-You Note Required" card KICKS ASS

1. Replaces a standard birthday/wedding/graduation card

2. Provides the receiver with the gift of time (the greatest gift of all)

3. Adds significant value to the actual gift

4. Saves the recipient the expense of a thank-you card

5. Reduces the amount of expected etiquette in this world

6. Angers traditionalists and uppity, pretentious assholes (always fun)

Something I Learned Today

"Mundanity" is a real word.

FEBRUARY 2
8:15 AM

DAYS WITHOUT

Chocolate glazed doughnuts	0
Gum	0
Crying	0
Little Debbie Snack Cakes	0
Green vegetables	0
Flossing	36
Retail rage	0
Regret over quitting my job	0
Dad	5,734

FEBRUARY 3
5:00 PM

A New Chapter Picks of the Month for February
   The Martian by Andy Weir
   The Road by Cormac McCarthy (bad choice for expecting
      fathers who fear the worst at all times)
   The Book Thief by Markus Zusak (makes my Jewish wife
      happy to see it on the list)
   The Count of Monte Cristo by Alexandre Dumas (Edmond
      Dantès was the John McClane of his day)
   Silver Sparrow by Tayari Jones

What I wanted to be when I grew up
   An astronaut

The very last thing I want to be as an adult
    An astronaut

Reasons I hated *The Martian*
    Mark Whatley made me feel like less of a man

Addition to Dan's Laws of the Universe
    Making an astronaut-botanist as brilliant, brave, and good-
        looking as Matt Damon sets unreasonable expecta-
        tions for the rest of us.

FEBRUARY 4
7:45 AM

Notes regarding Bill Donovan phone call
1. Don't remember giving him my number
2. "I'm Dan. Not Danny."
3. A lot of coughing
4. "We got bingo on Friday."
5. "We"?
6. Just filed his "fucking taxes."
7. His dead wife was a florist named April.
8. Cat named Pavlov
9. "You golf?"
10. "What the fuck do you do?"
11. Doesn't read books. "Just newspapers and billboards."
12. Lives alone (except for cat)
13. "*Wheel of Fortune* and *Jeopardy!* and all those fucking shows are for numb nuts."
14. "So you coming?"

15. "People who show up late suck at life."
16. "Get a fucking stamper."

FEBRUARY 4
9:20 AM

Things I just realized about Bill's call
1. "What the fuck do you do?" is a very good, very hard question.
2. A cat named Pavlov is funny.
3. What is a stamper?
4. Bill might be lonely.
5. Bill might know that I'm lonely.

FEBRUARY 5
2:20 AM

Questions I want to ask Jill but am afraid to ask
- Do you love me more than or less than the day we were married?
- Do you ever wish that I was your dead husband?
- How does my penis compare to Peter's penis?
- How many times a day do you think of your dead husband?
- How often do you regret marrying me?

Dan's Universe Law of Marriage (for Dan Only)
Life would be so much easier if I hadn't married Jill, but life would be so much harder if I hadn't married Jill.

FEBRUARY 5
2:55 AM

Charles Darwin's Pros and Cons of Marriage

MARRY

Children—(if it Please God)
Constant companion, (& friend in old age) who will feel
    interested in one
Object to be beloved & played with
Better than a dog anyhow
Home, & someone to take care of house
Charms of music & female chit-chat
These things good for one's health
~~Forced to visit & receive relations~~ *but terrible loss of time*

NOT MARRY

No children, (no second life), no one to care for one in
    old age
Freedom to go where one liked
Choice of Society & *little of it*
Conversation of clever men at clubs
Not forced to visit relatives, & to bend in every trifle

Dan's Pros and Cons of Marriage

MARRY

- Continued—albeit less than regular—sex for the duration of your life (presumably)
- A knowledgeable source more than willing to pause and explain the complex plots of television shows without judging you
- Household chores cut in half (more than half if you play your cards right)
- Guaranteed brunch companion
- Passenger to elaborate upon GPS directions while you're driving
- Naked woman walking around the house constantly
- Permanent wedding, Valentine's Day, and New Year's Eve date
- No more fear of STDs (or condoms)
- Someone to whisper the names of all the people you forget as they approach

NOT MARRY

- Just one stupid calendar to worry about instead of two
- You'll never wonder if your spouse's unwillingness to have sex on a given night is reflective of how much she loves you at that moment
- Change bedsheets a lot less frequently
- Guilt-free Wendy's spicy chicken sandwich for dinner any night you goddamn want it

- Hampers remain hampers and not not-so-temporary closets and bureaus
- Lights turned off in unoccupied rooms
- Avoid family gatherings by lying about "previous plans" without the fucking morality police questioning you
- Financial ruin is your own

FEBRUARY 6
7:18 AM

Why I won't stock Etch a Sketches in the store no matter what Jill says
- The Etch a Sketch makes me feel stupid.
- The Etch a Sketch is stupid.
- Paper and pencil are better.
- Drawing a picture of a fucking rectangle isn't supposed to be this difficult.
- The Etch a Sketch is bullshit.

FEBRUARY 6
3:22 PM

Things I am forever grateful for:
1. Growing up without the Internet
2. No more faculty meetings
3. *Buffy the Vampire Slayer*
4. Free refills
5. The ocean

6. Public ban on smoking
7. Vaccines
8. Bruce Springsteen
9. Little Debbie Snack Cakes
10. Peter's infertility
11. Lack of digital photography when I was in high school

FEBRUARY 6
6:40 PM

Text messages from Bill
> There is a football game on tonight. You should watch it. Expand your horizons.
> You get old unless you get new.
> You're too fucking young to be so fucking old already.
> Cross-stitching. And I love it.
> Did you see that sack?
> What's a sack?
> Fuck you.

Googled
> Sack: quarterback (or another offensive player acting as a passer) is tackled behind the line of scrimmage before he can throw a forward pass

Also Googled
> Line of scrimmage: the imaginary line separating the teams at the beginning of a play

FEBRUARY 7
7:18 AM

Things I Procrastinate About
    Clicking on my banking app
    Conversations with my wife about hampers
    Starting my diet
    Investing in an index fund
    Redesigning the children's section of the store
    Any chore involving a phone call

FEBRUARY 7
10:20 PM

Bingo with Bill
    "I told you to bring a stamper."

Doesn't smoke

"Never smoked. I always thought pizza and girls were better than cigarettes, so that's where I spent my money."

Plays nine bingo cards faster than I can play one

Asks lots of questions

"I hate these fuckers who complain about a fixed income. Lots of people are living on a fixed income. It's called minimum fucking wage, and it's criminal."

Bill walks and talks like a Republican but might be a Democrat

"No offense, Danny, but you quit teaching to sell books? What the fuck were you thinking?"

"Please tell me you at least got your pension first."

Shouts "Bingo!" like he's annoyed about winning

"You know about Amazon. Right? You know they sell books. Right?"

"If this book thing doesn't work, go back to teaching. Run back. Hard work is good work."

FEBRUARY 8
11:45 AM

Rules I Try to Live By
- I need to be impressed by you before I have the desire to impress you.
- Rules without consequences are merely suggestions.
- Deadlines without consequences are just lines.
- Always balance the cost of completing something stupid with the penalty for not completing it.
- Penalties rarely have any real teeth.

FEBRUARY 8
7:30 PM

Questions I asked myself today
1. Is the tightness in my chest from stress, a heart attack, or both?

2. Am I really going to do this?
3. How can $20,000 be a fortune for one person and a drop in the bucket for another?
4. When does a fetus know that it exists?
5. Is it better to eat a 250-calorie Twix or a 345-calorie avocado?
6. Was reading bad writing really so bad?
7. Why didn't I fight Jimbo Powers that day if I wasn't afraid to lose?
8. How hard would it be for me to get another teaching job?
9. Each penis can't be the same, so do women have clear and distinct memories of specific penises that they have encountered in their lives?
10. Do people who denigrate 7-Eleven hot dogs without ever trying one know that they are judgmental pricks?

FEBRUARY 8
11:05 PM

Five ways to say "movie" that say a lot about you
- Picture: Pretentious beyond measure
- Film: Marginally elitist
- Movie: Normal and decent
- Flick: Self-important and dismissive
- Motion picture: Serial killer

FEBRUARY 9
11:05 PM

Two Kinds of Teachers
    Those who loved school as a child
    Those who hated it

My Favorite Kind of Teacher
    Those who hated it

FEBRUARY 9
11:30 PM

New things so I don't get old
    Write a screenplay
    Learn to play the ukulele
    Cross-stitch
    Poker
    Soap carving
    Ventriloquism
    Learn to roller-skate

FEBRUARY 9
11:50 PM

Five ways I'll know that I've finally made it as a Hollywood screenwriter
    1. I write a movie wherein the male lead is wearing glasses and researching something and his female

romantic interest reminds him about the importance of eating.

2. I write a movie wherein the male lead has been treated for serious injuries and attempts to get out of bed in order to save the day, only to be pushed back by his female romantic interest, who reminds him that he is still recovering from that thing that would've killed any normal person.

3. I write a movie wherein alcoholism is a disease limited only to men and can be cured by the need to save the world.

4. I write a movie wherein mechanical failures can be instantly repaired with punches, kicks, head butts, and the pounding of wrenches to parts of the machine that have nothing to do with the failure.

5. I write a movie wherein the intelligence of law enforcement officials is inversely proportional to their rank.

Addition to Dan's Laws of the Universe

Everyone thinks they can write a screenplay, but in truth, almost everyone is only marginally good at complaining about screenplays.

FEBRUARY 10
12:20 PM

Things Peter Would've Never Said

"I think I'm going to try soap carving."

"Look at my ventriloquism dummy. Isn't he cool?"

"I cross-stitched you a throw pillow."

FEBRUARY 10
3:17 PM

Complaints received at the bookstore this past weekend
1. "You don't carry enough editions of the Bible."
2. "I can't believe you've never heard of the 'good guy discount.'"
3. "That redheaded lady is not very nice."
4. "What the hell is wrong with having a men's room *and* a women's room?"
5. "Twenty dollars? Do you realize that I could just check this book out of the library?"
6. "This winter sucks. Snow or get off the pot. Know what I mean?"
7. "Why don't you have a cat? Every good bookstore has a cat. You need a fucking cat."
8. "C'mon, man. If you're not selling coffee, you're not even trying."
9. "Your toilet paper sucks."

FEBRUARY 10
4:35 PM

Text messages from Jill
I'm a good teacher. Right?
Jasper doesn't seem to think so.
I know he is, but he's my boss, too. His opinions matter.
Thanks, honey. Love you.
I'm a good teacher. Right?

FEBRUARY 11
6:17 PM

My teaching beliefs
1. If you haven't given your students an authentic reason to learn, don't even bother teaching the lesson.
2. The most effective tool for assessing student progress is absolute honesty.
3. When it comes to discipline, you must only say things that you are willing to do.
4. The first step to planning every lesson is to determine how it will be fun for students.
5. Teachers must be reading and writing on a regular basis in order to be effective teachers of reading and writing.
6. The student's voice should be heard far more often than the teacher's voice.
7. Teachers must think of parents as full and equal partners in the education of the child.
8. If your students are not laughing at least once every hour in your classroom, you have failed them.
9. The most important lessons taught by teachers often have little or nothing to do with academics.
10. The best administrators understand that teachers are more knowledgeable about instruction than they could ever be.
11. Time is more valuable in the classroom than anywhere else in the world. Waste not a second.
12. It is almost impossible to set expectations too high for students.

13. The single greatest assessment of a teacher's effectiveness is their students' desire to come to school every day.

FEBRUARY 11
6:35 PM

Truths

I could've been a good teacher.

I should've been a good teacher.

I thought teaching would be easy, and that's why I failed.

I could still be a good teacher. Maybe.

Jill is a better teacher than I will ever be.

FEBRUARY 12
9:15 PM

Revised interview procedure (to weed out someone like Kimberly in the future)

1. Interview the last five people who served the candidate in a restaurant. Inquire about how the candidate treated them over the course of the meal.

2. Interview the candidate. Ask the following questions:

   • Please explain the Bill of Rights to your best ability.

   • Name as many Supreme Court justices as possible.

   • Tell me about the last three books you read.

- Tell me about one goal or aspiration that you have yet to achieve.
- Are you a good person?

Actual interview procedure used to hire Kimberly
1. When do you want to start?

FEBRUARY 13
4:00 PM

Questions I asked myself today
Could I get a bank loan?
Would Jill need to be involved with the application for a bank loan?
Why am I so excited about the alternative to a bank loan?

FEBRUARY 13
5:05 PM

What the Road Runner cartoons taught me
- Explosives are simple to deploy, easy to target, and never result in collateral damage.
- Vengeance should always be as violent as possible.
- Gravity is a fickle mistress that will momentarily cease to function if the end result is humorous and fucks you over.
- Acme is the only company on the planet.
- Coyotes can't be killed. Only flattened and blackened.

Addition to Dan's Laws of the Universe
> Solutions are a hell of a lot easier when you're the only one in need of saving. Also, explosives help too.

FEBRUARY 13
9:35 PM

ACTUAL COMPLAINTS RECEIVED BY "THOMAS COOK VACATIONS" FROM DISSATISFIED CUSTOMERS

1. "They should not allow topless sunbathing on the beach. It was very distracting for my husband who just wanted to relax."
2. "We went on holiday to Spain and had a problem with the taxi drivers as they were all Spanish."
3. "We booked an excursion to a water park but no one told us we had to bring our own swimsuits and towels. We assumed it would be included in the price."
4. "The beach was too sandy. We had to clean everything when we returned to our room."
5. "Although the brochure said that there was a fully equipped kitchen, there was no egg-slicer in the drawers."
6. "It took us nine hours to fly home from Jamaica to England. It took the Americans only three hours to get home. This seems unfair."
7. "I compared the size of our one-bedroom suite to our friends' three-bedroom and ours was significantly smaller."

8. "We had to line up outside to catch the boat and there was no air-conditioning."
9. "I was bitten by a mosquito. The brochure did not mention mosquitoes."

Actual complaints received THIS WEEK ONLY from dissatisfied customers
1. "I know it's what actually happened, but it's still weird that Anne Frank just stopped writing. Right?"
2. "I wish I could get God to sign this Bible."
3. "The problem with long books is they take longer to read."
4. "*The Da Vinci Code* should be in the *T* section. All books starting with the word 'the' should be in the *T* section. It only makes sense."
5. "You need a cat. Also coffee. Also lower prices."

FEBRUARY 13
10:55 PM

4 Rules I wish I could impose in the bookstore
1. Check your cell phone and your shoes at the door.
2. Purchase three books for every one toy purchased.
3. You drool on it, you buy it.
4. "We'll get that one at the library" will result in immediate tasering and relinquishment of all cash.

FEBRUARY 14
8:03 AM

MY VIEW ON PETER'S FEBRUARY 14 LETTERS

30%	Want to read
30%	Don't want to read
40%	Wish Jill had kept them a secret all along

ALSO . . .

100%	Wish they didn't exist at all

ALSO . . .

100%	Wish they weren't Valentine's Day letters

FEBRUARY 14
6:20 PM

2018 Letter
   Shorter than last year's letter
   Addressed to "My love"
   Signed "Love always"
   "I hope you've found love again."
   Story about their first roller-coaster ride together

Fudge ripple ice cream

"Say hello to my brother."

"Those damn slippers . . ."

Rein's Deli

"Has the world gone to hell in a handbasket yet?"

Good news

Jill didn't cry

Didn't say, "I'll love you forever" for the very first time in these letters

No mention of sex or Jill's body (like in 2014)

Only three years of letters left

Bad news

I acted like a fucking jerk when she asked me if I wanted to read it.

I corrected a dead man by saying it was "hell *and* a handbasket."

I was wrong. It's "hell in a handbasket."

Jill probably cried later.

Next steps

Never order fudge ripple ice cream again

Avoid Rein's Deli whenever possible

Avoid roller coasters whenever possible

Eradicate the expression "hell in a handbasket" from my vocabulary for as long as I live

FEBRUARY 15
3:22 PM

Phone calls
   Substitute teachers make $72 per day
   A bank loan is out of the question
   Cat litter is bad for pregnant women
   Enrollment is declining. Class sizes shrinking. No one had
      unprotected sex during the recession.

FEBRUARY 15
10:55 PM

8 things I don't miss about teaching
   1. Bullshit circle games by administrators who claim
      to treat teachers as professionals but then schedule
      teamwork activities with beach balls and candy
   2. Teachers who spend more time designing bulletin
      boards than reading good books
   3. Parents who insist that their average or above-average
      child is gifted
   4. Teachers who believe that titles "Mr." or "Mrs." confer
      some kind of artificial authority
   5. Teachers who speak to students in one voice and adults
      in another voice
   6. Teachers who dress up for parent–teacher conferences
   7. Administrators who run meetings as if their staff
      members are students
   8. Listening to people who no longer work with kids tell
      us how to work with kids

FEBRUARY 15
11:20 PM

Things I said to my students that were true but questionable

"There are no stupid questions. Just stupid people who ask questions."

"If you put things in your mouth other than food, you will have no friends."

"I won't punish you. I'll just reward everyone around you for not being you."

"Shame is an effective, long-lasting deterrent, and I will use it."

"You're not going to believe this: I put on two pairs of underwear today."

Truths

I've accidentally worn two pairs of underwear on more days than I'll ever admit.

I thought that accidentally wearing two pairs of underwear was funny, but I might be the only one.

After the third time, I didn't think it was funny anymore.

FEBRUARY 16
9:36 AM

Deep Economic Thoughts of Dan

1. Private school is the ideal means of exacerbating the growing economic inequality in America while creating

racial segregation and a glass floor for children who already have all of the advantages.

2. Therapy is a treatment that is both affordable and accessible to white people with health insurance, two-car garages, and time enough to worry about their problems.

3. Shops that close at 5:00 on a weekday are perfectly designed for intentionally unemployed women.

4. Serving on charitable boards is not the same as having a job that requires you to work every day in order to eat.

Additions to Dan's Laws of the Universe

It's so easy to despise the wealthy (or wealthier) when you are running out of money.

When you can send your kids off to private school and send yourself to therapy twice a week, you should be able to handle a little hatred from those less fortunate.

FEBRUARY 17
5:20 PM

Notes from VFW #2 (VFW Post 7788, Milford)

1. 2 doors—front and back. Unlocked. Maybe a kitchen door?

2. 80+ players
   a. All men.
   b. Table of serious-looking 40-year-old guys in back corner
   c. About one-third are disabled with canes or wheelchairs.
   d. So many cigars

3. $75 buy-in—all cash—$6K total pot
4. All cash collected at the door. Lockbox.
5. Highway on-ramp less than a quarter mile away

Thoughts:
1. I could've grabbed that lockbox and run. So damn close to the exit.
2. Less than half the cash of the South Street VFW, but so much easier. Risk/reward calculations are hard.
3. Why do these guys play bingo in silence? No one talks to one another.
4. I still need a bingo stamper.
5. I miss Bill.

Unsolved problems
1. Getaway vehicle?
2. Gun?
3. Alibi?

Truths
1. I'm terrified.
2. I feel so fucking alive.
3. I haven't felt in such control of my life in a long, long time.
4. I'm not sure if I'm brave enough to pull this off.
5. I'm having so much fun planning this.
6. A lockbox is a stupid and pointless thing if it can be picked up and carried away.
7. A "getaway car" is also a "get there" car.
8. Why is this so fun?

FEBRUARY 18
9:49 AM

Revised List of Fears

Good afraids
  Sharks
  Botulism (dented cans)
  Losing Jill
  Losing the store
  Losing the house
  Prison
  Erectile dysfunction
  Death
  Drunk drivers
  Hypodermic needles
  Dad walking into bookstore unannounced
  Butt crack sweat on my pants
  Icicles

Bad afraids
  Taking huge risks
  Tasting new foods
  Asking girls on dates in high school
  Driving into New York City
  Asteroids (not the video game)
  Sinkholes
  Asparagus pee
  Airplanes
  Verbal confrontations
  Public speaking

Only times I'm afraid of airplanes
1. When I'm flying in an airplane
2. When an airplane is flying over me

Most underestimated danger in the world
A plane falling out of the sky and landing on your head

Worst parts about my airplane fear
1. It's the height of narcissism to think that the exceptionally rare plane crash will someday happen to me.
2. It's hard to cry on a plane without being noticed.

FEBRUARY 19
9:49 AM

Text messages from Jill
Jasper is a dick.
He's making my days sad.
I know. But you don't know what it's like anymore.
He has favorites, too. Single women. Young.
Pauline. Maybe Amy.
I'm just going to keep my head down and hope he gets fired
or promoted soon.

FEBRUARY 19
9:56 AM

Husband problems
I can't punch Jill's boss in the face.
I can't force her boss to treat her better.

I feel like a little boy when I ask if she wants to have sex.
I don't understand how to handle her pregnant body.

Jasper (Jill's principal and my former principal)
    Liar
    Narcissist
    Tiny waist
    Steely Dan fan
    Enormous, fragile ego (worst combination ever)
    Three ferrets
    Constantly quotes self-help books
    Threatened by the success of his teachers
    Also has a pregnant wife
    Only eats "good barbecue"
    Loves to talk about "good barbecue"
    Probably thought that professional wrestling was real as a kid
    Constant, lewd comments to women, including Jill
    Coffee breath
    Can't swim
    Plays squash
    Needy as fuck
    PhD who insists upon being called "Dr."

Question
    I couldn't fight Jimbo Powers. Why do I think I could fight
        Jasper Berceuse?

Possible addition to Dan's Laws of the Universe
    No one really changes. Assholes are always assholes. Angels
        are always angels. You are the person you've always been.
        Some people just learn to hide their ugly parts.

More questions

    Is that true? I think it's true.

    If it's true, what does it say about me?

    Do people think about shit like this as much as I do?

    Does writing all this stuff down make it more real for me? More painful?

    More in need of answers?

    Should I stop these lists for my own sanity?

    Could I stop these lists and remain sane?

    Why does everyone like *Friends* so goddamn much?

FEBRUARY 19
10:55 AM

The worst people in the world

    Serial killers

    North Korean supreme leaders

    Drivers who obey the NO TURN ON RED sign when no car is coming for miles

    Librarians who think they own the books

    Westboro Baptist Church

    Ferret owners

    Hecklers

    Facebook comment-baiters

    People who prolong meetings with stupid questions or questions pertaining only to them

    Line cutters

    People who play Monopoly using bullshit "house rules"

    Large, fragile egos

Drivers who purposely take up two parking spaces
People who don't ever read
Confident idiots
Steely Dan fans

Four stupidest things that principals do

1. Park in PRINCIPAL'S PARKING spot
2. Not ending meetings early
3. Speaking more than listening
4. Complaining about the amount of time required to handle a problem or crisis

Three investments that school districts should make to improve learning

1. Hire or train staff who can teach teachers in engaging, informative ways
2. Tear down every fucking bulletin board and tell teachers to spend their time reading good books and planning lessons that make kids laugh instead
3. Eliminate all administrative positions between principal and superintendent

Why ferrets are stupid pets

1. They smell
2. They poop at least 10 times a day with the consistency of brown toothpaste
3. They are uncivilized, vicious little fuckers
4. They are almost impossible to walk
5. You look like a jackass while trying to walk them
6. They're a stupid, disgusting form of a cat, so just get a cat

7. They are vehicles for attention-seeking pet owners
8. College girls think they're cute for about six minutes, then you have to spend two months finding someone stupid enough to take them off your hands

FEBRUARY 20
7:45 PM

Things I learned in birthing class
    No Wi-Fi in the birthing center
    Bring food (this could take a while)
    Vaginal birth is horrific
    Stay above the equator at all times
    The birthing center validates parking
    Sex can stimulate labor
    Don't Google image search *anything* related to childbirth
    Don't go to the hospital too early or you will be sent home
    Women who have babies in the back of taxis make this all seem a lot easier
    We have 24 hours after the water breaks to deliver the baby
    A woman's sense of self-worth seems oddly and inexorably connected to her use of pain medication during the birth of her child

New Questions
1. How can we have sex if there is a sack of water waiting to be broken in the vagina?
2. Is an episiotomy what I think it is?

3. If an episiotomy is what I think it is, how the hell did it get its name?
4. What percentage of fathers hate their children (even a tiny bit) for what they did to their wives' vaginas while being born?
5. Is it a terrible idea to Google "episiotomy"?

FEBRUARY 21
6:15 AM

Ben Franklin's List of Virtues
1. TEMPERANCE. Eat not to dullness; drink not to elevation.
2. SILENCE. Speak not but what may benefit others or yourself; avoid trifling conversation.
3. ORDER. Let all your things have their places; let each part of your business have its time.
4. RESOLUTION. Resolve to perform what you ought; perform without fail what you resolve.
5. FRUGALITY. Make no expense but to do good to others or yourself; i.e., waste nothing.
6. INDUSTRY. Lose no time; be always employ'd in something useful; cut off all unnecessary actions.
7. SINCERITY. Use no hurtful deceit; think innocently and justly, and, if you speak, speak accordingly.
8. JUSTICE. Wrong none by doing injuries, or omitting the benefits that are your duty.
9. MODERATION. Avoid extremes; forbear resenting injuries so much as you think they deserve.

10. CLEANLINESS. Tolerate no uncleanliness in body, cloaths, or habitation.
11. TRANQUILLITY. Be not disturbed at trifles, or at accidents common or unavoidable.
12. CHASTITY. Rarely use venery but for health or off-spring, never to dullness, weakness, or the injury of your own or another's peace or reputation.
13. HUMILITY. Imitate Jesus and Socrates.

Franklin's virtues I espouse
ORDER. Let all your things have their places; let each part of your business have its time.

Note: Hampers are not a place for clothing.

CLEANLINESS. Tolerate no uncleanliness in body, cloaths, or habitation.

Note: Hampers of clean clothing makes my habitation unclean

Franklin's virtues I desperately need
RESOLUTION. Resolve to perform what you ought; perform without fail what you resolve.

TEMPERANCE. Eat not to dullness; drink not to elevation.

Note: In fairness, stress-eating isn't the same as eating to dullness (whatever the fuck "eating to dullness" means)

Proof that Franklin had a giant stick up his ass
1. He wrote this list at age 20.
2. He tried to "live without committing any fault at any time."

3. He focused on one virtue each week and kept notes on his progress.

Truth (seriously)

Writing lists is kind of the same as focusing on a virtue a week and keeping notes on progress (in that it might be obsessive and possibly crazy)

FEBRUARY 22
12:00 PM

Advantages of A BIKE!
1. Car can stay behind to provide alibi
2. Not restricted to streets
3. Easy to dump
4. Can be purchased cheaply with cash

Disadvantages
1. Not nearly as fast
2. I don't ride very well

New questions
1. Where could I leave my car to establish an alibi?
2. Can I ride a bike at night?
3. Could I carry the money while riding the bike?
4. Is it true that once you know how to ride a bike, you can always ride a bike? Even after 15 years?

FEBRUARY 23
4:30 PM

Letters sent today
  Bill and Melinda Gates Foundation
  440 5th Ave N.
  Seattle, WA 98109

  Warren Buffet
  3555 Farnam St.
  Omaha, NE 68131

  Mark Cuban
  5424 Deloache Ave.
  Dallas, TX 75220

  Jeff Bezos
  Evergreen Point Road
  Medina, WA 98039

Reasons given for donation
  1. Teacher and bookshop owner
  2. Pregnant wife
  3. Literal drop in the bucket for them
  4. Enormous self-satisfaction
  5. Visible beneficiary
  6. Eternal gratitude
  7. 25% discount for life at A New Chapter (meant for a
     laugh)

Important note on language
   "Bookshop" = quaint, privately owned
   "Bookstore" = corporate, soulless

FEBRUARY 24
7:05 PM

Things Jill thinks but doesn't say
   1. Why can't Dan fix the garage door? Or replace a flat tire? Or hang a picture frame?
   2. He still can't load a dishwasher correctly. Unbelievable.
   3. His mother is a pain in the ass.
   4. I wish my husband had a hobby.
   5. A hamper makes a perfect bureau.
   6. Why can't he just masturbate tonight?
   7. Peter was better-looking.

FEBRUARY 25
4:45 AM

Places to purchase a bike
   Trek Bicycle
   Craigslist
   Tag sale
   Dick's Sporting Goods
   Play It Again

FEBRUARY 27
4:45 AM

Favorite sentences

- "But what is happiness? It's a moment before you need more happiness."—Don Draper
- "In a world where superheroes, and more importantly super-villains, exist, being a glazier must be a great job."—Michael Maloney
- "He was the fourth of three children."—Daniel Mayrock
- "The saddest of all the ribbons is the white ribbon." —Unknown
- "None of us marry perfection; we marry potential." —Elder Robert D. Hales

FEBRUARY 27
8:20 AM

Shopping List

Always goddamn dog food
Raspberries
Toilet paper
Bingo stamper
Goldfish
Diet Coke
Little Debbie Snack Cakes
Kettle ball still
Powerball tickets

FEBRUARY 27
8:45 AM

Why raspberries are a bullshit food
- They last for about 14 minutes before devolving into mush
- Less than two dozen berries in a package
- Only fruit that needs to sit on a diaper
- The silent *p* makes them impossible to spell

FEBRUARY 27
8:55 AM

Products that I'd better get the brand right when shopping or Jill will kill me
- Toilet paper
- Shampoo
- Bar soap
- Laundry soap
- Tissues
- Milk

** Basically milk plus anything that touches her body

FEBRUARY 27
9:23 AM

Deep thoughts related to food
1. There is no way that anyone can taste the difference between 1% and 2% milk.

2. Little Debbie Snack Cakes last at least 500 raspberry lifetimes, <u>and that's a good thing</u>.

3. Everyone complains about preservatives and processed food until the apocalypse, and then they'll all be on their knees thanking the food industry for canned creamed corn and Twizzlers.

4. I don't believe any human being has ever purchased a can of creamed corn.

5. If you're going to more than one grocery store in a week, you have too much time on your hands and have somehow elevated the quality of your heirloom tomatoes over time spent with your family.

FEBRUARY 27
1:10 PM

Three hours with Bill Donovan

- I'm apparently going to be "Danny." I'm afraid to correct him.
- It oddly doesn't bother me.
- Same clothes as last time. Exactly same clothing. Tweed pants. Blue button-down. Brown loafers.
- "Bingo is bullshit. A lot of shit is bullshit."
- Angry, but not nearly as angry as he's trying to be. Funny. I think he might be funny.
- "I like bingo because it's mindless. Sometimes you just don't want to think about the things you've done."
- I think Bill played bingo for the same reason people are still watching *Friends*.

- Still coughing
- Thinks that people who eat lobster are "fucking morons"
- His father died of cancer. "It started in his gut and ate right through him."
- "No, she didn't die of fucking cancer."
- "Don't apologize. I'm the asshole. Not you."
- My father ~~is~~ was the only other person who calls me Danny.
- "The problem with bingo is that the waiting to win is better than winning. I sit here, hoping I win, but it's the hope I want. Not the money. You know what I mean?"
- Don Draper and Bill have the same definition of happiness.
- "Who chooses whiskey over beer? Guys who drink the hard stuff don't like themselves. They're either trying to be something they're not or running from something they don't want to be."
- His wife was murdered in a carjacking gone wrong. Shot three times. Just said it plain as day after getting another beer. *Fuck.*
- "After Vietnam, I never thought I'd want to die. But I wish I had died first. April could've had a life after me. I'm not a second act kind of guy. I'm still stuck in my first act."
- Bill is exactly my father's age.
- "When your wife dies, people look at the space where she used to be instead of at you."
- "Fuck me. Bingo!"

FEBRUARY 28
6:30 AM

Greatest Hits

Spring 1992: Caught my one and only fly ball in a Little League baseball game

Summer 1996: Walked the beach with Melissa Zarizny. She definitely liked me. I definitely fucked it up.

Spring 1997: Track and field district championships: fourth place in the pole vault

Summer 1997: Lost my virginity to Kami Norris in New Hampshire in the Bat Cave (her closet/bedroom)

Summer 1997: Completed Dragon's Lair at the Half Moon Arcade in Weirs Beach, New Hampshire

July 4, 1998: Beat Jake in arm wrestling at the family picnic at Candlewood Lake

August 1998: Sex with Jenny on 18th green at Quarry Ridge

May 1999: Full scholarship to University of Connecticut

April 2001: Second place, student council presidential election, University of Connecticut

October 2002: Op-ed in *Hartford Courant* on the truth about the 98.6 degree "normal" temperature

June 2006: Hired by West Hartford Public Schools

September 2006: Made Jill laugh in a faculty meeting

July 4, 2009: Jill says yes to my proposal

July 1, 2013: Open the bookstore

Thoughts on Greatest Hits
- Quite a few of my greatest hits involved women and sports, even though the two things I have never excelled at are women and sports.
- Why didn't I write another op-ed after "98.6 degrees is fiction, just like carrots are good for the eyes"?
- My mother's most common question in 2002 was: "When are you going to write another thing for the paper?"
- There's been nothing close to a greatest hit since I opened the store.
- Listing my greatest hits did not make me feel as good as I had hoped.

FEBRUARY 28
8:14 AM

Addendum to Thoughts on Greatest Hits
- It only took me 14 years to ask myself the same question my mother was asking me in 2002.

FEBRUARY 28
8:30 AM

Addendum to the Addendum on Thoughts on Greatest Hits
- I hate when my mother is right. Even more than a decade later.

MARCH

Finances
    Savings: 2,803

Income
    What I tell Jill: nothing
    Reality: 930
    Jill: 2,900

Expenses
    House: 2,206
    Toyota: 276
    Honda: 318
    Car insurance: 175
    Student loans: 395
    Cable and Internet: 215
    Electric: 132
    Oil: 446
    Phones: 180
    Gas: 101
    Crib: 479
    Goddamn armchair apparently required for nursing: 689
    Infant car seats (because we apparently need TWO): 622

MARCH 1
5:23 AM

Changes Since Jill Became Pregnant
    Doesn't ask about the store's finances *at all*
    Clarence not allowed on the bed anymore
    A lot of steamed vegetables at dinner
    Antimicrobial everything

MARCH 1
7:15 AM

Financial Solutions

REALISTIC

- Bingo

PIPE DREAMS

- Begging billionaires (letters sent)
- "No Thank-You Note Required" greeting card

"No Thank-You Note Required" To-Do List
    1. Design a prototype
    2. Make a prototype
    3. Worry about everything else after I have a prototype

MARCH 1
8:00 AM

DAYS WITHOUT

Chocolate glazed doughnuts	20 (approximate)
Gum	31
Little Debbie Snack Cakes	0
Flossing	67
Retail rage	2
Regret over quitting my job	0
Dad	5,759

MARCH 1
4:30 PM

3 reasons why I am a terrible man
1. I'm jealous of the time Jill spends at Peter's grave on the anniversary of his death
2. I'm annoyed about the money she spends on flowers for his grave
3. I secretly wish each year that she'll forget about today

MARCH 2
9:05 AM

A New Chapter Picks of the Month for March
Underground Airlines by Ben H. Winters

The World According to Star Wars by Cass R. Sunstein (Star Wars shit always sells)

Rules for a Knight by Ethan Fucking Hawke

Hillbilly Elegy: A Memoir of a Family and Culture in Crisis by J.D. Vance (even though I didn't finish . . . He made his point halfway in)

If This Isn't Nice, What Is?: Advice for the Young by Kurt Vonnegut

The Baker's Daughter by Sarah McCoy

MARCH 2
11:00 AM

People who I hate for being too accomplished
1. Ethan Fucking Hawke
2. That actor/comedian from *The Office* who was also a writer for *The Office* and that book of short stories and that perfect kid's picture book with no pictures (I really hate that guy)
3. Adele
4. Matt Damon
5. Anna Kendrick

People I should hate for being too accomplished but can't because I love them too much

Bruce Springsteen

Carrie Fisher

Nora Ephron

MARCH 2
5:50 PM

Unexpected things I did today
Didn't eat a Little Debbie Snack Cake
Spoke to Peter while alone in the office
Cried while speaking to Peter
Called Jake

What I said to Peter
I'm sorry.
I'm trying my best to take care of Jill.
Sometimes I wish you were still here to take care of Jill.

MARCH 2
5:55 PM

Things Jake said on the phone call
- "Are you okay?"
- "You never call. That's why."
- "Is it Jill?"
- "I'm sorry."
- "Yes, I'm happy."
- "Did you really call to ask me this? I've got barbecue on the grill.
- "No offense? How can that be no offense?"
- "Here's the thing: When you're a kid, you dream about your dream job because you can't see anything else.

But then you find your dream girl, and the job isn't as important anymore. Not even close. It's just the thing that lets you get back to your dream girl. Then you have a kid and forget it. You just want to get home to those two people."

- "I grew up. We all do."
- "I don't know if you can do both."
- "Are you sure you're okay?"
- "Don't do anything stupid."
- "I'm kidding. You're the last one in the world to do anything stupid."

MARCH 3
4:20 AM

Lies I Tell Jill

The store is more profitable than it really is.

I never miss teaching.

I'm happy that Peter is "still in our lives."

I love Clarence.

My therapist wants me to keep on writing lists.

Steve isn't very bright.

It would be great if the baby brought my father and me back together.

I'm fine.

I voted for Obama the first time.

MARCH 3
10:00 AM

6 Ways to Annoy a Child
1. If asked, declare that you have no favorite number.
2. If asked, declare that you have no favorite color.
3. Refuse to divulge your own middle name.
4. Ask a child how many fingers they have. When the child says ten, point out that they only have eight because two of their digits are thumbs. Then seriously question the child's intelligence.
5. Say popular catchphrases in the most robotic and uninspired way possible while pretending like you are trying your best to say the phrase properly.
6. Explain that the unicorn is not an imaginary animal but an extinct animal. Use the existence of the narwhal, the rhino, and all other horned land animals to support your assertion. Hold on to it like a dog to a bone.

MARCH 4
7:00 PM

Words that I hate
- Lover
- Frenemy (actually just an enemy)
- Norms (a favorite of administrators with nothing productive to say)
- Flaccid (it means "to hang loosely or limply," but it really only means one thing)

- Meh
- Fart (it makes me think of a butthole)
- Stakeholders (better referred to as "people who give a shit")

MARCH 5
8:00 AM

Two Kind-of-Serious Business Ideas

1. Informative diapers: Instead of *Sesame Street* characters on diapers, how about messages for parents on how to help your child succeed?
2. Life Capture: A company that aggregates texts from an individual, a couple, or a family in order to save for posterity

Possible diaper messaging

Sing to your child. Try the ABCs or "The Itsy-Bitsy Spider."

Put down the phone, numb nut.

Research says you shouldn't allow this precious child to watch any screens for the first two years of life.

Don't even think about taking this baby into a movie theater.

Remember this: When your baby is screaming in a restaurant, that is why they invented "outside the restaurant."

Read to this precious child every day. Even at an early age, reading makes a huge difference. It will decrease your child's chances of living at home as an adult.

If your child is still sleeping in your bedroom at the age of two, you suck at boundaries.

New word that I hate (and hate myself for using)
Messaging

MARCH 6
11:40 AM

Important Culturally Related Questions
1. Why does Carly Rae Jepsen think it's crazy that a girl might give a guy her phone number after just meeting him? Isn't this how dating works?
2. I don't care what the Lord of the Rings nerds say: Why didn't the eagles just bring Frodo to Mordor? Or better yet, why didn't Tolkien just make Frodo and Sam hike back home through a literary montage and avoid this eagles bullshit?
3. "They say in heaven, love comes first"? Really, Belinda Carlisle? When was this ever said, and who is *they*?
4. Rachel Platten is not correct. Truth is not what you believe in. This is the problem with the fucking world. Truth is no longer fact-based.
5. Why would anyone drink Mr. Pibb?
6. Why doesn't Doc Brown just tell Marty and his girlfriend what is going to happen to their kids in the future so they can just avoid the trouble altogether?
7. I'm supposed to clap along if I feel "like a room without a roof"? What is that supposed to feel like? Incomplete? Exposed to the elements? Topless?

Addition to Dan's Laws of the Universe

Musicians get away with a lot of shitty, illogical, nonsensi-
cal lyrics because they are writing their songs for stupid
teenagers and mindless conformists.

Lyrics that make total sense and are the shit

"The Gambler" by Kenny Rogers

"Code Monkey" by Jonathan Coulton

"Stan" by Eminem

"Suspicious Minds" by Elvis

"Ob-La-Di, Ob-La-Da" by the Beatles

"She's in Love with the Boy" by Trisha Yearwood

"The Star-Spangled Banner" by Jimi Hendrix

"A Boy Named Sue" by Johnny Cash (written by Shel
Silverstein)

"I Am a Rock" by Paul Simon

"Thunder Road" by Springsteen

Songs that you would think have great lyrics but don't

"American Pie" by Don McLean (sorry, Don, but some of
that doesn't make sense)

"Cats in the Cradle" by Harry Chapin (see it coming a mile
away, no surprise) (also prefer the Ugly Kid Joe version)

Truths

I would never tell Jill that I prefer Ugly Kid Joe to Harry
Chapin.

If Jill preferred Ugly Kid Joe to Harry Chapin, it would
somehow be cool.

MARCH 7
7:20 AM

Phone call from Bill

"Why don't you ever call me?"

"For fuck's sake. Watch a goddamn basketball game so we have something to talk about."

"Nothing's as big as it seems unless someone's dying. Or dead."

"You didn't think to tell me she's pregnant? What the fuck?"

"No fish and no booze. You know that. Right?"

"You got time on Tuesday afternoon? I need a ride."

What I want to talk to Bill about but can't

I want to be someone.

I want to be brave.

I want to be better than Peter.

I want my dad to be proud of me.

I want to be the kind of man who can take care of Jill.

I want to do something.

I don't want to be just another ordinary person in an ordinary life.

Mistakes

Thinking the bookstore would make me less ordinary

Believing that I could turn the business around

Lying to myself that the business was turning around

Lying to Jill that the business was hugely profitable

Not being more of everything and less of nothing

Truths
    Bingo would be something
    Not sure if it would be a good something
    It wouldn't be an ordinary something
    It solves a lot of problems
    Not just money problems

MARCH 7
11:00 AM

Kurt Vonnegut's outstanding redefining of the seasons
    January and February: Winter
    March and April: Unlocking (we're definitely in the un-
        locking. Nothing about today is spring)
    May and June: Spring
    July and August: Summer
    September and October: Autumn
    November and December: Locking

MARCH 7
2:45 PM

Things I'm loving
    Chipotle burritos
    Kottke.org
    Lyle Lovett Pandora station
    My wife in a T-shirt and underwear
    Cold water from a metallic water bottle

Carhartt socks in place of slippers
Egg McMuffins
Hoodie
Any day over 35 degrees

MARCH 8
10:13 PM

Worst news

World hunger still exists.

Cancer has not been cured.

Jill's breasts are now painfully sensitive.

MARCH 8
11:50 PM

Rules for Life in London (Rudyard Kipling, 1908)

1. Wash early and often with soap and hot water.
2. Do not roll on the grass of the parks. It will come off black on your dress.
3. Never eat penny buns, oysters, periwinkles or peppermints on the top of a bus. It annoys the passengers.
4. Be kind to policemen. You never know when you may be taken up.
5. Never stop a motor bus with your foot. It is not a croquet ball.
6. Do not attempt to take pictures off the wall of the National Gallery, or to remove cases of butterflies from

the National History Museum. You will be noticed if you do.

7. Avoid late hours, pickled salmon, public meetings, crowded crossings, gutters, water-carts, and over-eating.

Rules for Life in West Hartford (altered slightly from Kipling's list)

1. Wash early and often with soap and water. Hot water is unnecessary (scientific fact) and wastes money.

2. Roll in the grass. Cling to the joys of childhood as long as possible because adulthood is impossibly problematic unless you're someone like my brother who always seems to fall ass-backward into good fortune, or a trust-fund baby who has somehow avoided substance abuse and overall dickishness. Also, the world is no longer coated in coal dust (despite the best efforts of some politicians), so don't worry about your dress.

3. Never use your cell phone as a telephone on public transportation, in movie theaters, or in restaurants. It annoys people and makes them want to kill you. Also, empty the goddamn hampers immediately. They are transport vessels. Not storage vessels.

4. Be kind to policemen. Apparently nothing has changed in terms of law enforcement since Kipling's day.

5. Never play croquet. It's a stupid, elitist game (as demonstrated in *Heathers*).

6. Do not attempt to take pictures off the wall of the National Gallery (or any museum), or to remove cases

of butterflies (or any other object) from the National History Museum. You will be noticed even more so today than in Kipling's day because there are cameras everywhere. Big Brother rules the world. George Orwell was right. If you even try to remove anything from a museum, you will definitely be arrested. Also, doing so will make you an asshole.

7. Avoid late hours, pickled salmon, crowded crossings, gutters, over-eating, and all meetings of every kind.

MARCH 9
12:20 AM

Note

Animal Farm was published 9 years after Kipling died.

MARCH 9
1:50 AM

Middle-of-the-night realization

Amazing, mind-altering, immortal books like *Animal Farm* will be published after I am dead, meaning there will be books that I will never be able to read and never even know existed. Seems obvious, but until I dreamt about Kipling missing out on *Animal Farm* by nine years, it never really hit me like this. How awful for Kipling. And for future dead me.

MARCH 9
8:20 AM

To Do
    Don't ever die.
    Read faster.

MARCH 10
3:45 PM

Notes from prenatal visit #2
- Nothing is wrong with Jill or the pregnancy or anything, so why am I so nervous every time we enter that doctor's office?
- Jill gained six pounds.
- Jill can pee in a cup at any moment. I don't know how she does it.
- Jelly on belly.
- Nothing I say in that exam room is as funny as I think it'll be.
- Baby heartbeat.
- Tears.
- The constant pinching on Jill's left side is a ligament stretching. Her entire body is changing so she can squeeze this baby out.
- You'd think that evolution would've made childbirth easier for women.
- Evolution is patriarchal.
- Cystic fibrosis test negative.

• Met the male ob-gyn in the practice. There's no way he's not a creepy asshole.

MARCH 10
4:40 PM

Surest signs that Jill still loves me
1. She carries on a conversation with me while peeing with the bathroom door open.
2. She'll scratch my back forever if necessary.
3. She holds my hand in the movie theater.
4. She drapes her leg over my body while I sleep.
5. She'll still listen to Meatloaf in the car with me when I know she hates the music with every fiber of her being.

MARCH 11
10:55 AM

Surest signs that I still love Jill
1. I don't want her to ever worry about anything ever again.
2. I say nothing about the hairs in the sink.
3. I wash my hands before dinner even though I think it's stupid.
4. I only complain about the hampers once or twice a week.
5. I still have moments when I can't believe that she is my wife.

6. I used to want to be something for me, but now I want to be something for her even more.
7. It hurts to lie to her.
8. I listen to her describe her faculty meeting in detail without complaint or disinterest.
9. I am so afraid of losing her.

MARCH 11
2:40 PM

Text messages from Jill

I'm starting to feel the same way about meetings that you do.

Then I remember we met in one of these fuckers, and all is forgiven.

Mostly.

It really sucks when your boss doesn't trust you to do the simplest things.

Why can't he just do his job and leave us alone to do ours.

MARCH 11
2:43 PM

Truths

The missed question mark was Jill. Not me.

I thought about correcting her for half a second.

I thought about correcting it here for about two minutes.

I'll still be thinking about correcting it three days from now.

MARCH 11
3:30 PM

Rules of meetings that leaders never understand
- The shorter meeting is always the best meeting. Ending on time means you're not highly effective. Just average.
- Ending late means you suck at life.
- A meeting without laughter is a failed meeting.
- Providing everyone with a clicky pen at the beginning of a meeting is lunacy.
- The reviewing of norms before a meeting is a clear indicator of a lack of confidence in your ability to lead.
- If you can't conduct your meeting without an accompanying PowerPoint presentation, you should not be conducting a meeting.
- "Let's start off with an icebreaker" are words no human being has ever wanted to hear.

Addition to Dan's Laws of the Universe
A birthday party without a cake is just a meeting.

MARCH 11
6:00 PM

14 Reasons People Cannot or Will Not Delegate Responsibilities (and therefore become awful administrators who make my wife and her colleagues insane)
1. They possess an unwavering belief in "one right way."
2. They cannot accept any less than 100% of their expectations being met.

3. They lack faith in the capacity of others.
4. They fail to understand the importance of autonomy when delegating responsibilities.
5. They fail to recognize the value of an initial investment of time in future productivity.
6. They do not plan ahead.
7. They do not maintain a to-do list (mentally or physically).
8. They cannot think open-endedly.
9. They are ineffective teachers.
10. They value work over results.
11. They view a reduction in their workload as a threat to their ego or self-worth.
12. They fear failure.
13. They are overly attached to habit or routine.
14. They do not follow up on the delegated in productive and inspiring ways.

The Reasons I Cannot Delegate Effectively
1. I'm kind of afraid of my employees.

MARCH 12
3:45 PM

New baby stuff
- Jill has a baby bump.
- Jill's baby bump is surprisingly sexy.
- Strollers cost a fucking fortune.
- Car seats are bullshit. Fucking expiration dates?

- Cribs cost two fucking fortunes.
- Diapers. Holy shit.
- Cloth diapers are specifically made for self-loathing parents and those parents who have the time to make parenting their career and want us all to know it's their career.
- A crib *and* a cradle?
- Nesting is a real thing.
- Why are parents paying for *Sesame Street* characters on their diapers when the babies don't care and only shit and piss all over them?
- A chair specifically purchased for nursing is a made-up thing.
- I should sell baby shit instead of books.
- Babies are a fucking racket.

MARCH 12
10:40 PM

Notes from Chesterfield Fire Company Bingo Night
1. Second floor—one exit. Firetrap. Irony not lost on me.
2. Irony apparently lost on every other person in that place.
3. 100+ players
   a. All men. Ages 30–70.
4. $50 buy-in—all cash—$5K total pot
5. Could not determine where the pot is held prior to payouts
6. Firemen are huge. Even the retired ones.

Thoughts:
- No way. The layout sucks and the guys scare the shit out of me.
- I hate bingo. It is so fucking stupid.
- I can't use a theme song if I'm riding a bike as my "get there" and "get away" vehicle.
- I keep waiting for me to bail on this ridiculous and insane idea, but every day I like it more and more.
- "Thrilled" and "frightened" are like Siamese twins. You need one for the other.

Unsolved problems:
1. Gun?
2. Burial site

MARCH 13
4:30 PM

Bill's appointment
- "Can you drive me to an appointment?" means "Can you spend most of the day waiting with me?"
- "No, I'm not fucking dying. What is wrong with you?"
- "There's nothing embarrassing about a wart unless you're eight years old and stupid."
- Bill dresses up for his doctor's appointments. Tie and cardigan. Looks like an old man.
- "Your wife's a widow? Fuck. You don't tell me? Are we friends or not?"
- Bill is my friend.

- Knows receptionist by her first name
- Handicapped parking is amazing
- I have no idea why Bill is handicapped.
- "What's with the pen and paper? Fuck. Are you writing a book? Or the longest fucking grocery list in the history of the world?"

"What You Need to Understand About Your Wife" according to Bill (who has never met her)

- Her heart is big enough to keep loving her dead husband and love you, too.
- There are days when your wife's dead husband will be more alive to her than others, and you need to be a special kind of prick to not allow her that.
- Don't try to compete with a dead man. The dead man always wins because he can't fuck up anymore.
- It takes guts to marry a widow. Unless you didn't realize that it took guts. In that case, you were just dumb.
- It's hard to love again. Don't forget that. She married you, so she must really fucking love you.

Additions to Dan's Laws of the Universe

Four hours in elderly person's time = five minutes in their mind.

It's okay to refer to parking as "handicapped" but people are disabled (until that term is deemed offensive), which makes no sense except that all those parking spots already have the signs.

If you replace the phrase "Americans think" with "Americans who own landlines who answer unsolicited calls think" the world makes a lot more sense.

Contents of waiting room
  24 chairs
  2 coffee tables
  6 copies of *Good Housekeeping*
  4 copies of *Time* magazine
  4 human beings (not including me and Bill)
  One coatrack

Addition to Dan's Laws of the Universe
  The ratio of chairs to patients in waiting rooms is seriously
  fucked-up.

MARCH 14
9:00 AM

Current Hierarchy of A New Chapter staff
  Kimberly: Thinks she's in charge (and sends me angry
    emails alluding to this)
  Steve: Allows Kimberly to be in charge when he is actually
    in charge (smart)
  Jenny: Doesn't give a fuck about being in charge
  Sharon: Smart enough not to want to be in charge
  Robby Hugh (regular customer who never buys anything):
    Acts like he's in charge
  Me: Supposedly in charge but failing miserably

A tweet that seemed to be written specifically for me and also ridiculously aspirational

> "Reminder that Winnie the Pooh wore a crop top with no panties, ate his favorite food, and loved himself and you can too"

MARCH 14
1:45 PM

9 lowest forms of human communication
1. The demanded apology
2. The absence-of-a-thank-you-note complaint
3. The "I'm angry at you and will write an email rather than speaking to you in person or calling you" email
4. The anonymous critique or attack, in any form
5. The read-aloud PowerPoint slide
6. Any meeting agenda item that could've been conveyed via email or memo
7. The disingenuous, disinterested "How are you?"
8. The weatherman reading temperatures on a map that we can clearly see
9. The personal tragedy one-upmanship

MARCH 15
11:30 PM

Notes from VFW #2 (VFW Post 7788, Milford) (second visit)
1. Confirmed door in kitchen—unlocked
2. 92 players (Bill's official count)

3. $75 buy-in—all cash—$7K total pot
4. Cash collected at the door. Same lockbox. Brought to back table after the game starts.
5. Cashier recognized me. Fuck.
6. Stamper makes things a lot easier.
7. Stamper makes it a lot easier to get ink on your clothing.

Thoughts:
1. There's a moment just before the first game starts when the lockbox is still at the table by the front door with one or two old guys sitting there. So easy to grab.
2. Why limit myself to just one job?
3. Using the word "job" makes me feel better about it.
4. I already can't believe how okay I feel about this.
5. I'll need a mask. So stupid. Hadn't thought about this until tonight. Ski mask?
6. I can't do this unless I'm 100% certain that I won't be caught.
7. 100% certainty won't be too hard, I think.
8. I had the same level of confidence about running a bookstore before actually running the bookstore.

Questions:
1. Why does Bill like me?
2. Bill likes me. Right?
3. Macbeth killed King Duncan only after his wife badgered him into committing murder. Am I better or worse than Macbeth for taking on this job on my own?

MARCH 16
2:40 AM

Worst part about this plan
1. Lying to Jill
2. Secrets from Jill
3. Not being able to sleep because I'm so nervous
4. Not being able to sleep because I'm so excited

Question
1. If you do something kind of amazing but can never tell anyone, is that enough?

MARCH 16
8:40 AM

Tag sale acquisitions
Paper towel holder
iPhone charging cables
Fishing pole and tackle box
Small bookcase
Bike

MARCH 17
6:00 AM

Why I hate St. Patrick's Day
It's just an excuse to drink (and get drunk)
I used to host huge parties for St. Patrick's Day when I was younger but now I don't

Green is a stupid color
Other nationalities don't get a day (except for the Italians
    and Columbus Day, which is stupid)
It's my father's birthday

MARCH 18
11:05 AM

57 sins listed by 19-year-old Isaac Newton while studying at
Trinity College in Cambridge

BEFORE WHITSUNDAY 1662

1. Using the word (God) openly
2. Eating an apple at Thy house
3. Making a feather while on Thy day
4. Denying that I made it.
5. Making a mousetrap on Thy day
6. Contriving of the chimes on Thy day
7. Squirting water on Thy day
8. Making pies on Sunday night
9. Swimming in a kimnel on Thy day
10. Putting a pin in John Keys hat on Thy day to pick him
11. Carelessly hearing and committing many sermons
12. Refusing to go to the close at my mothers command
13. Threatning my father and mother Smith to burne
    them and the house over them
14. Wishing death and hoping it to some
15. Striking many

16. Having uncleane thoughts words and actions and dreamese.
17. Stealing cherry cobs from Eduard Storer
18. Denying that I did so
19. Denying a crossbow to my mother and grandmother though I knew of it
20. Setting my heart on money learning pleasure more than Thee
21. A relapse
22. A relapse
23. A breaking again of my covenant renued in the Lords Supper
24. Punching my sister
25. Robbing my mothers box of plums and sugar
26. Calling Dorothy Rose a jade
27. Glutiny in my sickness.
28. Peevishness with my mother.
29. With my sister.
30. Falling out with the servants
31. Divers commissions of alle my duties
32. Idle discourse on Thy day and at other times
33. Not turning nearer to Thee for my affections
34. Not living according to my belief
35. Not loving Thee for Thy self.
36. Not loving Thee for Thy goodness to us
37. Not desiring Thy ordinances
38. Not long {longing} for Thee in {illeg}
39. Fearing man above Thee
40. Using unlawful means to bring us out of distresses
41. Caring for worldly things more than God

42. Not craving a blessing from God on our honest endeavors.
43. Missing chapel.
44. Beating Arthur Storer.
45. Peevishness at Master Clarks for a piece of bread and butter.
46. Striving to cheat with a brass halfe crowne.
47. Twisting a cord on Sunday morning
48. Reading the history of the Christian champions on Sunday

SINCE WHITSUNDAY 1662

49. Glutony
50. Glutony
51. Using Wilfords towel to spare my own
52. Negligence at the chapel.
53. Sermons at Saint Marys (4)
54. Lying about a louse
55. Denying my chamberfellow of the knowledge of him that took him for a sot.
56. Neglecting to pray 3
57. Helping Pettit to make his water watch at 12 of the clock on Saturday night

Notes on Newton's List
- Isaac Newton was a fucking menace.
- "Striking many" is an unjustly nonspecific, especially given "Beating Arthur Storer"

- "Punching my sister" and "Making pies on Sunday night" don't belong on the same list.
- What makes Dorothy Rose a "jade"? Also, what the fuck is a jade?
- "Using Wilfords towel to spare my own" is the most fucked-up thing on the list. Complete assholery.
- It's probably worth suffering at the hands of Isaac Newton if you get your otherwise forgotten name recorded for posterity (Dorothy Rose, Arthur Storer)

MARCH 18
11:35 AM

Steve's thoughts on Newton's list
- Thinks "Putting a pin in John Keys hat on Thy day to pick him" is the worst sin on the list. "That's serial killer shit."
- "Newton would've played on defense. They're all terrible human beings."
- "Striking many is not cool, but it sounds pretty badass, too."
- "Is 'Squirting water on Thy day' what I think it is?"

MARCH 19
12:50 PM

Dumbest things said to me today by customers
"You should sell the movie version of the book instead. It's a lot better than the book."

"Did you know that *Playboy* was the first gentlemen's magazine to be printed in braille? It's also one of the few magazines with colorized microfilm. So you might want to carry it."

"I'm looking for a blue book. Tiffany blue. It's about a woman, I think. My book club is reading it. The reviews are terrible. Have you read it?"

Smartest things said to me by a customer today

"It's hard to hate a person with a book in their hand."

"I just had lunch at Taco Bell, and it was great. I don't care what my husband thinks. I love him, but he can be such a fucking snob sometimes."

MARCH 19
1:30 PM

Prenatal visit (20 weeks)

- No, we haven't felt the baby move.
- By "we," we mean Jill.
- Amount of time between "No, we haven't felt the baby move" and "That's totally normal" was entirely too fucking long.
- Jill has gained 12 pounds. The doctor says it's "fine," which means it's not, and I want to kill him for it.
- "Any abdominal fullness, gas, belching, discharge, or heartburn?"
- Jill tells every doctor and nurse—even the ones not

examining her—that we don't want to know the sex of the baby.
- They must think she is a crazy person.
- I think she is a crazy person.
- Baby is the size of "a medium-sized banana pepper."
- Fundal height is six inches.

Amniocentesis

Jill decided not to prep me on the definition of an amniocentesis

Jill calls it an "amnio" like they've been friends forever

Jill probably assumed that I know what an amniocentesis is

My thought: "Why would we take a chance on losing the baby for information that changes nothing?"

I think that saying those words out loud made Jill happy

Things I didn't say

What the fuck is a banana pepper?

Is "fluid retention" caused by not peeing enough?

What is fundal height?

Do I have a fundal height?

Whatever fundal height is, it sounds disgusting.

Are there really parents who would abort their little banana pepper for something as manageable as Down's?

Addition to Dan's Laws of the Universe

It's wrong to judge a parent's reproductive decisions, but it's less wrong to silently judge them in your head.

MARCH 20
7:20 PM

Number of customers before 3:00 PM today
   2

Number of customers after 3:00 PM today
   6

MARCH 20
8:45 PM

Dinner with Jill
  • She eats a lot now.
  • Started knitting a hat for the baby.
  • Telling her that "We could just buy a hat" was not a great idea.
  • "Shyloh is bright and funny and talented, but she's at least two years behind her classmates. I don't know what to do."
  • Jill has at least two dozen Shylohs. Every year.
  • She glows. I swear that pregnancy is making her glow. Also belches like she's never belched before.
  • "Jasper told me you can't save them all. That's why Jasper is a dickhead."
  • I agree. Jasper is a dickhead.
  • Jasper is also not wrong.
  • Bowling?

Proposed baby names

GIRLS

Clara
Caroline
Cassidy
Alice
Bella

BOYS

Jack
Brady
Charlie
Benjamin

VETOES

Brandon (my former student)
Monica (Jill's former student)
Stephanie (Jill's high school frenemy)
Cranberry (Jill doesn't like)

For the record

- I have no problem with that actress who named her kid Apple. I like that name a lot.
- I was serious about Cranberry.
- There's no need to laugh at a name just because you've never heard it before.

- Laughing at someone's idea is not nice.
- Choosing a permanent name for a human being who you've never met is hard.

MARCH 20
9:32 PM

Addition to Dan's Laws of the Universe
>Just because something is true doesn't make it okay to say it.

MARCH 20
11:45 PM

Stupid names for schools
>Northeast Academy
>Northwestern University
>Northwest Academy
>Schools named after the street they are on (basically a hat on a hat)

Additions to Dan's Laws of the Universe
>Just because you're naming a child doesn't mean the naming of other things can't help you in the naming of a child.
>Studying the stupid way of doing things is helpful when trying to find the smart way to do things, even if your wife thinks it's not.

MARCH 21
9:15 AM

The only times in life when we should allow someone to dictate what we wear without paying us for our time
- When we are children
- When attending the work function for a significant other
- When we're asked to serve as a bridesmaid or groomsman or pallbearer

MARCH 22
3:16 PM

Personal schadenfreude
1. Watching people fail to parallel park on the first try
2. Technology failures just prior to or in the middle of important presentations
3. Kirk Cameron's *Saving Christmas* as the worst-rated movie ever on IMDB
4. Salad eaters' inevitable regret over not ordering the burger
5. Seeing high school asshole and smug valedictorian Payton Sommers washing dishes at the Chicken Shack at age 38.
6. Parking tickets for people who don't buy anything in the store

MARCH 23
4:45 AM

Things I wish I'd known when I was young

1. Never be afraid to talk to the prettiest girl in the room.
2. Always talk to the prettiest girl in the room.
3. The prettiest girl in the room is not necessarily the prettiest person.
4. Wait to purchase your ideal home. There is no reason to rush into such a large purchase. Cherish the joys of apartment living.
5. Dance often. Dance to songs you both love and loathe. Just dance.
6. Reasonable people can disagree.
7. Don't gossip. Nothing makes you look uglier.
8. When in doubt, never wash any item of clothing owned by a woman.
9. Do the thing you are thinking about doing right now. Today. Thinking about it is simply fear masquerading as thoughtfulness.
10. Living well is the best revenge. If that doesn't work, bide your time. You can always ruin your enemy's life at a later date.
11. Cherish those moments in your work life when your bosses and coworkers are in perfect harmony. They will not last forever.
12. Always assume that children are more capable than you think.

13. Make every attempt to befriend—or at least endear yourself to—your friend's spouse.
14. People with large, fragile egos are the most dangerous of all people.

MARCH 24
9:00 PM

Best parts of my day
1. Touching Jill's baby bump this morning
2. Texts from Jill
3. Another Bill phone call

Worst parts of my day
1. 10% increase in rent going into effect on June 1
2. Another letter from Dad
3. I ate six Little Debbie Snack Cakes in the back of the store like a criminal
4. I can't ride a fucking bike

Texts received today from Jill
I can't believe we're making a baby
I don't want to read *What to Expect When You're Expecting*. Let's be surprised. And I think it's probably all bullshit. Okay?
(Three heart emojis)
Be ready to fool around tonight
Can you grab bread on the way home babe

Why I'm an asshole
- I don't use emojis because I think they're stupid.
- I correct Jill's grammar and punctuation in her texts (in my head only).
- Jill's grammar and punctuation errors annoy me.
- I think slightly less of Jill for her texting errors.

Questions
- Do our texts get saved somewhere? Maybe for our baby to read someday?
- Would parents or kids want that kind of record of their lives?
- Would Jill be more diligent with her grammar and punctuation if they were saved for posterity?

MARCH 25
12:00 AM

Things that Don't Make Sense
1. People obsessed with the *Hamilton* soundtrack even though they've never seen the musical.
2. There are partitions between some urinals but not all urinals. We either need penis privacy or we don't.
3. Sophie la Girafe.
4. Paul Revere is remembered, but the guy who did the exact thing on the exact same night is forgotten (I've forgotten his name too).

Follow up after rereading the last list
1. I've never listened to the *Hamilton* soundtrack, but I still think I'm right.
2. I prefer partitions. I like penis privacy.
3. His name is William Dawes.

MARCH 26
7:20 AM

Useless skills
I can finger spell the alphabet with American Sign Language

I can recite about two dozen poems by memory, including three in French

I can accurately report on the plotlines of all seven seasons of *Buffy the Vampire Slayer*

I can shave with soap only and no mirror

Slightly less useless skills
Fall asleep within 30 seconds

I can sleep in almost any position in almost any location

I can hold my breath for a really long time

I have a poor sense of smell (and am therefore rarely bothered by odors)

I can swallow my anger

Lost skills
Standing on the seat of my bike while moving

MARCH 27
12:30 PM

People I admire
- People with doctorates who don't require or even ask for the use of the title
- Non-mechanics who can lift the hood of a car and determine what is wrong
- Fast readers
- Adults who don't pretend not to watch porn
- Name rememberers
- Men who play in softball leagues
- Steve
- Anyone who can walk into a Home Depot and purchase items without assistance
- Travelers who can pack everything into a carry-on
- Jill

People I admire but would never admit
- Jake
- Nixon pre-Watergate
- That guy from *The Office* who wrote that book of stories and that kick-ass children's book

MARCH 28
10:20 PM

Dinner with Mom
- Angry that we waited three months to tell her
- Only angry at me

"Order the ravioli, damn it. It's great. Don't you trust me?"

Likes baby names that start with hard consonants

Writing an op-ed on the need for more mimes in the world (not kidding)

Sort of offered to buy us a crib (I think)

"I've been saving lots of stuff in the basement for this day, but I gave most of it to your brother."

"I hope you have a birth plan."

MARCH 29
11:50 PM

The problems with the 40th birthday party for Jill's friend Wendy

- People who talk about alcohol like it's an interesting topic
- My inability to extract myself from a one-on-one conversation that has fizzled
- Sports talk
- The assumption that I can do sports talk because I have a penis
- My apparently senseless guilt over other people ignoring the live musicians and not even acknowledging when one of their songs ends
- People who chant, "Speech! Speech! Speech!" after the candles are blown out
- Jill leaving me alone among people I barely know
- Me feeling like a dick for feeling all these things

Question

When people chant, "Speech! Speech! Speech!" after the candles are blown out, do they really want to hear a speech? Have they been dying to hear what the birthday boy or girl has to say? Are they desperately awaiting words of awkward appreciation and a panoply of glittering generalities? Or is it just shit that they have seen in a movie reproduced in real life?

MARCH 30
5:30 PM

Sentences Spoken by Steve During Inventory
- "It's impressive. You own a bookstore and you're making a profit."
- "Belichick is a monster."
- "I'm looking for an opportunity. A way to do what you've done here. Build something. Make something. Thank God I have a wife who understands."
- "Every time I wipe my son's ass, I can't believe that my father did the same for me."
- "I'll never understand why people prefer fiction when the real world has so much to offer."
- "Maybe he didn't. Maybe Mom did all the wiping."

Googled
Belichick: Football coach

APRIL

Finances

Savings: 2,117

Income

A New Chapter: 1,322

Jill: 2,900

Expenses

House: 2,206

Toyota: 276

Honda: 318

Car insurance: 175

Student loans: 395

Cable and Internet: 215

Electric: 98

Oil: 0

Phones: 180

Gas: 100 (approximate)

APRIL 1
12:15 PM

If I ruled the world, 9 laws that I would immediately enact

1. Drivers who pull their cars alongside each other in the middle of the road and roll down their windows in order to chat (thus blocking the road for sane people) shall have their licenses revoked for a period of no less than 5 years.

2. If a public building has two or more exterior doors, all such doors shall be accessible and open at all times. If a patron walks into a door expecting it to open and finds it locked, the business in question shall pay the patron a fee of $50,000. If said patron bashes his or her head on the door in the process (a feat I have accomplished several times), ownership of the business shall immediately be transferred to the bloody-nosed patron.

3. Anyone wearing an article of clothing containing a brand name or any assemblage of words on the seat of his or her pants shall be required to remain seated for the rest of his or her natural life.

4. It is hereby forbidden to congratulate a friend on the purchase of a vehicle if that friend exceeds the age of eighteen. When the purchase of an automobile becomes congratulatory-worthy, priorities must be reexamined immediately.

5. When going to the gym, one must drive to an open parking spot and park your car immediately. No more occupying-the-middle-of-the-aisle, directional-flashing minivan lunatics (it's always a minivan) waiting for that prime spot ten feet from the doors.

6. It is no longer permissible to refer to any article of clothing as "fun." You sound ridiculous.

7. If more than half of your social media posts pertain to your latest fitness or nutritional regimen, you are hereby banished to Google+ for a period of no less than one year.

8. Selfie sticks are immediately banned. It's bad enough that future archaeologists may judge our society based upon things like *The Bachelor*, Steven Seagal, and hipsters who wear slouchy winter hats in the summer. We cannot allow the selfie stick to also define us.

9. People who pay by check at the grocery store must take a mandatory class on the safe and effective use of debit and credit cards before being allowed to eat any of the groceries that they have purchased.

APRIL 1
5:00 PM

Items on Panera bulletin board by the restrooms
Sedgwick Middle School production of *Aladdin*
Friday night open mic at Playhouse on Park
Business card for Fishman Hardwood Flooring
Bingo at Daughters of the American Revolution

Two thoughts
Daughters of the American Revolution has a bingo night.
Has a business card on a bulletin board ever resulted in any business ever?

APRIL 2
9:20 AM

A New Chapter Picks of the Month for April
>   *Rabbit: The Autobiography of Ms. Pat* by Patricia Williams
>   *Vacationland: True Stories from Painful Beaches* by John
>   Hodgman
>   *1984* by George Orwell and *The Dead Zone* by Stephen
>   King (combo seems apropos)
>   *Manhattan Beach* by Jennifer Egan (haven't read yet but as-
>   sume it's great)
>   *Lincoln in the Bardo* by George Saunders

APRIL 2
12:10 PM

11 Things that Annoy Me
1.   People who live in the suburbs of a city but claim resi-
     dence to that city
2.   Drivers who fail to understand that NO RIGHT ON
     RED really means BE CAREFUL BEFORE MAKING YOUR
     PERFECTLY LEGAL RIGHT ON RED
3.   Continuous discussions about body ailments and/or
     illnesses
4.   The recounting—word for word—of conversations that
     are clearly only interesting enough to warrant para-
     phrasing
5.   The massive stores of memory lost forever when a per-
     son dies

6. The almost universally incorrect use of the phrase "Begs the question"
7. A New Yorker's way of saying "on line" instead of "in line"
8. The bizarre pride that some New Yorkers feel (and openly express) about saying "on line" instead of "in line"
9. Songs about specific people that are named after those specific people (Elton John's "Daniel," Journey's "Amanda," Eric Clapton's "Layla")
10. The muddy, cold brown days between winter and spring (unlocking)
11. Almost every rhetorical question ever asked

APRIL 2
2:14 PM

Daughters of the American Revolution flyer
  Third Friday of every month
  7:00 PM
  $10 cover/$100 to play
  West Hartford Town Hall

Information not included
  Number of players?
  Cash only?
  Ladies only?
  Daughters of the American Revolution only?

Phone call plan
> Calling on behalf of my mother
> Open to the public?
> Will she need cash?
> Can I bring my mother?

APRIL 2
9:22 PM

Solutions
> Getaway: Bike
> Identity: Ski mask
> Location: Daughters of the American Revolution

Still a Problem
> Gun

Gun
> I don't like guns
> I've never owned a gun
> I don't want to own a gun
> I don't know how to buy a gun
> I don't know how to load a gun
> I don't want to use a gun
> I don't want to frighten anyone with a gun
> I don't want to frighten myself by using a gun

New questions
- How can you convince people to hand over their money without a weapon?
- Why can't this be more like an *Ocean's Eleven* movie? None of those guys used guns, I think.

Addition to Dan's Laws of the Universe
Robbing a casino with a dozen of the world's greatest con men isn't exactly brave or even risky. *Ocean's One* . . . now that would be a movie.

APRIL 3
2:20 AM

Amazing octopus facts as learned on YouTube when I should be sleeping
They have three hearts.
They're the only invertebrates capable of using tools.
They can change their color in less than a second.
They can open childproof pill bottles.
There are three plural forms of "octopus": "octopuses," "octopi," and "octopode."
They don't have a centralized brain.

Additions to "Things I Can't Do"
I can't use tools.
I have a really hard time opening childproof pill bottles.

Addition to Dan's Laws of the Universe
> The octopus is far more impressive than I will ever be. No matter what I do in this world, I'm a human being with thumbs and a giant brain and the collected knowledge of centuries of human existence in my pocket. Given my advantages, nothing I do will ever be as amazing as an octopus opening a childproof pill bottle.

APRIL 3
4:15 AM

Enormous Musical Mistakes
> I thought "Under the Boardwalk" was originally recorded on Bruce Willis's *The Return of Bruno* album.
> I told Jill that Meatloaf was one of my favorite musicians.
> I thought "(Sittin' On) The Dock of the Bay" was a Michael Bolton original.
> I chose the flute in third grade.
> I attended a Creed concert in the mid-nineties.

APRIL 3
9:45 AM

Text messages from Bill
> Are you having a boy or girl?

> I want to get you a gift, numb nuts.

> I'm impressed.

Most people can't delay gratification for a second these days.

If you had one of those fucking pink or blue gender-reveal party things, I would've had to punch you in the face.

Surprises are good. We don't get enough of them in this life.

And most surprises stab you in the fucking heart.

APRIL 3
7:18 PM

Today's totals
    $163 in sales
    At least twice that in salary paid
    1 parking ticket (Jill)
    2 customer complaints
    14 Jill belches (that I heard)
    2 Little Debbie Snack Cakes
    1 pool of vomit (toddler)
    1 new hamper of clothing (3 total)
    2 sensitive breasts

Complaints
    "If you installed hand dryers, I wouldn't have to stare at that PLEASE DON'T FLUSH PAPER TOWELS DOWN THE TOILET sign every time I use your bathroom. It makes me sad for humanity."

Kimberly, to a customer who was upset that the book he ordered hadn't arrived yet: "Listen, mister. Just because your day isn't cheery doesn't mean you should try to ruin mine."

Addition to Dan's Laws of the Universe
> There is never a need to tell a person to listen to you if that person is three feet away and staring at you.

APRIL 3
11:55 PM

Rules of Manhood
- Stop talking about where you went to college.
- You will regret your tattoos.
- When in doubt, always kiss the girl.
- You may only request one song from the DJ.
- Measure yourself only against your previous self.
- Revenge is an excellent cure for anger.
- No one cares if you are offended, so stop it.
- Read more. It allows you to borrow someone else's brain, and will make you more interesting at a dinner party.

APRIL 4
12:20 PM

Weird Things I Do
> I don't look at the pilot when boarding a plane in fear that he will remind me of an idiot who I know.

> I always take a leaflet from people handing them out because I like to think that they can finish sooner and go home if I do, even though that's probably not true.

I speak to houseflies. I warn them that they only have three days in this world. Three days before death. I warn them that they need to make the most of the little time they have. I'm fairly emphatic about it.

My thumbs do a little dance over the phone when I'm not sure how to reply to a text.

When I am alone, I drive with the windows down, the heat or AC blasting depending upon the season, and the music at full volume. Loud enough to make people stare.

Whenever I find myself adjacent to a brick wall, I reach out and touch a brick, knowing that a bricklayer once placed this brick, and all the rest around it, into the wall.

I purposely attempt to cut every corner in every hallway in order to shorten the distance between the two points and perhaps recapture a little lost time.

I plant pennies heads up because of the commonly held superstition that finding a penny on heads is good luck and/or allows you to make a wish.

APRIL 4
12:40 PM

Things I Will Never Do

Refer to myself as old or make one of those "I'm officially old" jokes because calling yourself old is the first step to becoming old

Get a haircut on the same day as the event that requires the haircut

Get another dog after Clarence dies

Skydive

Order food in a restaurant by saying, "I'll do the chicken marsala."

Start using hand lotion (huge scam)

Facts about skydiving

Skydiving is safer than driving a car, but you generally don't see your death coming in a car accident like you do in skydiving, and that makes all the difference.

I grudgingly promised Jill that I would never skydive.

I have never, ever wanted to skydive but pretended to agree to Jill's compromise in hopes that it might make me appear brave.

The youngest skydiver ever was four years old, but that doesn't mean that he was brave. He just had assholes for parents.

APRIL 5
11:10 PM

Notes from Daughters of the American Revolution Bingo (West Hartford Town Hall, Main Street, West Hartford)

1. No smoking. Huzzah!

2. Multiple exits to outside and interior of town hall
    a. Two sets of double doors to town hall interior
    b. One set of double doors to outside
    c. Two single doors to stairwells to second-floor wrap-around balcony
    d. One door onstage, behind the curtain, to town hall interior
3. West Hartford Center directly outside
    a. Shops
    b. People
    c. Movie theater
    d. Library
    e. Parking garage
    f. Fucking parking meters
4. 200+ players
    a. Women
    b. Two men
    c. Average age: 60? (Women's ages are hard)
5. $10 cover charge/$100 buy-in—all cash—$20K total pot
6. Open bar
7. Money is held onstage in an unlocked? lockbox
    a. Three women (middle-aged or older) sitting stage left behind a table with lockbox
    b. Two women (middle-aged) sitting center stage, calling numbers
8. Daughters of the American Revolution is lineage-based, which makes it exclusionary, elitist, and snobby, which makes it feel better to hit

Questions

1. Can I just disappear into the crowd on the streets?
    a. If so, where do I hide the money?
2. Can I disappear into the town hall and exit one of the exterior doors?
3. Are any parts of the town hall alarmed?
4. Are there security guards in the town hall after hours?

Thoughts

1. This could work.
2. I have never been so afraid in my life.
3. I have never been so excited in my life.

Truths?

I was an average teacher. Maybe an average husband. A bad bookstore owner. A jealous brother. The worst son. Maybe this is a thing I can do well.

I'm doing something that Peter could never do.

I'm doing something.

I feel like someone.

Maybe I've watched too many heist movies.

It feels so good to be brave.

APRIL 6
3:13 AM

Jonathan Swift was 32 when he wrote this advice to his future self.

WHEN I COME TO BE OLD. 1699.
Not to marry a young Woman.

Not to keep young Company unless they reely desire it.

Not to be peevish or morose, or suspicious.

Not to scorn present Ways, or Wits, or Fashions, or Men, or War, &c.

Not to be fond of Children, or let them come near me hardly.

Not to tell the same story over and over to the same People.

Not to be covetous.

Not to neglect decency, or cleenlyness, for fear of falling into Nastyness.

Not to be over severe with young People, but give Allow-ances for their youthfull follyes and weaknesses.

Not to be influenced by, or give ear to knavish tatling ser-vants, or others.

Not to be too free of advise, nor trouble any but those that desire it.

To desire some good Friends to inform me wch of these Resolutions I break, or neglect, and wherein; and reform accordingly.

Not to talk much, nor of my self.

Not to boast of my former beauty, or strength, or favor with Ladyes, &c.

Not to hearken to Flatteryes, nor conceive I can be beloved by a young woman, et eos qui hereditatem captant, odisse ac vitare.

Not to be positive or opiniative.

Not to sett up for observing all these Rules; for fear I should observe none.

Advice to my future self

Give your children space to shine

Do not complain about the same illness more than once in a single day

Offer advice in snippets lasting 30 seconds or less

Don't nag

Remember that old age does not give you permission to be a dick

Find things that your children do that you can be proud of, even when their accomplishments seem meager at best

Treat counter workers well

Do not favor one child over another

Don't interfere in your child's dating and spousal decisions

Don't be afraid to admit that you are hard of hearing

Don't stop having sex

Babysit my grandchildren whenever possible

Get out of the house every single day

Don't fall behind on technology

Don't watch reruns

Continue to find music that is new to you

Try like hell to surround yourself with people younger than yourself

Die before your wife and children

Use handrails

APRIL 7
5:00 PM

Stupid things said in the bookstore today
> (overheard) "You should spend that money on a nipple piercing instead."
> "Are all your books nonfiction?"
> "Did you know that Costco sells books cheaper than you?"
> (phone call) "Do you sell reading books?"

(overheard by Steve) "Hold on! I want to take a selfie with this because it has this guy who looks like Gordon Lightfoot on the cover."

(asked to Sharon) "What's your shortest version of *Huckleberry Finn*?"

Addition to Dan's Laws of the Universe

You should be required to read a book for every ten selfies you take.

APRIL 8
5:00 PM

Level 2:	Volkswagen Bug (yellow, elevator)
Level 3:	Corvette (under car cover)
	Subaru Outback (green)
Level 4:	Hyundai Tucson

APRIL 8
8:35 PM

Notes on fake guns

You can be convicted of armed robbery even when using a fake gun.

An unloaded real gun and a fake plastic gun are essentially the same thing during a robbery in the eyes of the law.

A finger under a shirt pretending to be a gun is the same thing as using a loaded gun.

Fake bombs are the same as fake guns except possibly worse (terrorism implications).

Addition to Dan's Laws of the Universe
There are no fake guns in the eyes of the law.

APRIL 9
11:20 PM

Three people I hate
1. Complainers: There is nothing wrong with taking is-
    sue in a matter of importance, but if you are a person
    who finds something to complain about on an almost
    daily basis, or you have several complaints going on at
    the same time, the problem is not the world. The prob-
    lem is you. And we all hate you for it.
2. Yeah, but: Similar to complainers, these are people who
    reject solutions to their problems by simultaneously
    acknowledging the potential effectiveness of a proposed
    solution while at the same time finding ways to con-
    tinue to complain about the same problem. These are
    people who enjoy problems and find simple solutions
    oddly offensive.
3. Escalators: These are people who may have legitimate
    issues with individuals, organizations, and other enti-
    ties, but rather than approaching these entities in a
    measured, productive, civil manner, they take pride and
    pleasure in airing out their issues in public or semipublic
    forums in ways that make everyone around them un-
    comfortable. These are also people who constantly as-
    sume the worst of others and love to threaten to sue
    at the drop of a dime.

Biggest problem with Kimberly
She's all three of these people rolled up into one.

APRIL 10
11:45 AM

Prenatal visit #3
Mother in waiting room tells hyperactive toddler son to "Pound sand."

Same mother tells Jill that her top is "fun."

I love my baby already, and I know my baby is coming, but it still doesn't seem real. Can't believe this thing growing inside Jill will someday drive a car and eat Chinese food.

Pee and sex and menstruation and babies all happen in the same basic area of a woman, making you wonder what the fuck Mother Nature (evolution) was thinking.

"Baby looks great." Three best words maybe ever.

I'm kind of obsessed with the male ob-gyn at the practice. How does that happen?

Doctor's offices need coat hooks and Wi-Fi.

How I imagine a male ob-gyn might justify his life choices
"I've wanted to work with vaginas ever since I was a little boy. It was my calling."

"The female form fascinates me."

"It's just a vagina. No different than an elbow or an eardrum, really."

"It's not like my wife's vagina. I don't get emotionally attached to the vaginas at work."

"Someone has to poke around vaginas. I figured, 'Why not me?' Right?"

"I tell my mother that I'm a pediatrician. It's easier that way."

Future plan

Find a way to tell someone to "Pound sand" this month.

APRIL 10
7:33 PM

The most despicable things that parents do to their children

Dress identical twins identically

Eliminate risk and stakes from a child's life through the proverbial parental bubble wrap and the construction of a glass floor that eliminates the possibility of failure via private schools, family businesses, and monetary bailouts

Put a child on a leash (literally)

Tell a child to "pound sand" (but this might also be amazing)

Insist on "helping" with school projects when help is not requested

Become overly involved in a child's clothing decisions

Fail to read to a young child every single day of his/her life

Leave it entirely in the hands of their child to remain in contact with their parents when they become adults

APRIL 11
5:40 AM

Things that are bullshit
    Bathrobes
    Green bean casserole
    Jill's "Last one to get out of bed makes the bed" rule
    Maypoles
    Art in restaurant bathrooms
    Throw pillows

APRIL 11
9:30 AM

Questions to ask at lunch without actually asking
    What should I do? About basically everything?
    How did you do everything right all the time?
    Can you save me?

APRIL 11
11:45 PM

Lunch with Mr. Sullivan
- He doesn't age.
- He still wears a jacket with patches on the elbows, even to a diner.
- I'm a grown-ass man, but somehow he's still my high school English teacher.
- "I guess if you're going to quit teaching, opening a bookstore is a noble alternative."
- He didn't cry, but he also didn't *not cry* when I told him that I decided to become a teacher because of him.
- Married for 32 years.
- *Six kids*
- Why do restaurants just assume that it's okay to place an unannounced pickle on my plate? Don't they realize how pickles contaminate everything with their insidious pickle juice?
- "I've read that it's incredibly difficult to make a profit from bookstores today. You must be doing something right."
- It hurts to disappoint your high school English teacher, even as a grown-ass man.
- He ordered a second cheeseburger after he finished the first. As casual as asking for a drink refill. I couldn't believe it.
- "It's a shame you missed out on your pension by just a couple years. Even 20% would've been nice."
- "Honestly, after the third, it stops mattering. It's sounds crazy, but six is basically the same as three.

- "You just do whatever it takes to keep your family happy and safe. It's that simple."
- "You can always go back to teaching, Daniel. There are always kids in need."
- Insisted on picking up the check.

Questions

1. Why didn't I read about how incredibly difficult it is to make a profit from a bookstore today before opening a bookstore?
2. I had a pension?
3. What is the point of the patches on the sleeves of sports jackets?
4. I wonder if any of my former students will invite me to lunch someday.
5. Why did I think that I could get the answers to my most important questions without actually asking them?
6. Will I ever get to the point where I can just order a second cheeseburger like it's no big thing?

APRIL 12
6:05 AM

When I knew Jill and I were perfect for each other
    We both eat our hot dogs plain.
    We both think that Swiper is the stupidest name for a television character whose primary function is to steal things from Dora the Explorer.

We don't believe in waffling our fingers when holding hands.

We both can explain net neutrality, credit default swaps, and the symbolism in *The Great Gatsby* in plain English.

Questions I don't dare ask

How did Peter eat hot dogs?

Does Jill avoid waffling our fingers because that was how she and Peter held hands?

How did Peter and Jill know that they were perfect for each other?

APRIL 12
8:45 PM

Reasons for fighting with Jill tonight

I told her kugel was a shitty food that Jews like only because they were indoctrinated to like it, and that if it was an objectively good food, it would be available in restaurants.

I said that her parents should probably stay in a hotel when they come to see the baby.

I proposed that no one be allowed to hold the baby until they admit that climate change is real.

I aggressively washed the dishes after she didn't wash them right away.

Hormones

APRIL 13
5:20 AM

Facts about the baby moving
> It moved.
> I saw it move.
> I felt it move.
> I will never forget it for as long as I live.

APRIL 14
5:45 AM

Facts about me after I saw and felt the baby move
> A baby doesn't start to exist for me until I saw evidence
> that the baby exists.
> I didn't know that my baby didn't exist in my mind until it
> started existing in my mind.
> Believing that my baby exists makes me a new kind of
> happy.
> Believing that my baby exists makes me a new kind of fuck-
> ing terrified.

APRIL 14
7:50 PM

Best decisions I ever made
> Staying off social media.
> Avoiding drugs

Migrating early from Internet Explorer
Sitting next to Jill in that faculty meeting
Seeing Tom Petty and Prince in concert before they died
Not proposing to Jill with that stupid airplane banner
Hiring Steve

APRIL 15
1:30 AM

More facts about me after I saw and felt the baby move
    I can't sleep.
    My baby deserves better.
    My baby is real. Not theoretically real but moving around real.
    I don't think I can go through with it anymore.
    I can't risk this baby not having a father like me.
    I can't be selfish or stupid anymore.
    Maybe being a father is enough.
    I'll find another way.

Addition to Dan's Laws of the Universe
    Babies make men want to be better human beings.

APRIL 15
9:00 AM

New solutions
    Tell Jill.
    Close the store and find a job.

Ask Mom for help.
Ask Jake and Sophia for help.

Problems with new solutions

TELL JILL:

- Doesn't actually solve the problem
- Makes me feel pathetic and weak
- She has too much on her plate already
- Peter never lied to her
- I've lied for so long
- I might lose her

CLOSE THE STORE AND FIND A JOB:

- Store makes a little money, so it's not a complete failure
- Closing now would cost me more money than it would save (initially)
- I've lied for so long
- I might lose her

ASK MOM FOR HELP:

- I would never hear the end of it
- She might not have enough money to save me
- Not a long-term solution
- She would tell Jake

- She might tell Jill
- I might lose her

ASK JAKE AND SOPHIA FOR HELP:

- I would never hear the end of it.
- They would tell Mom.
- They might tell Jill.
- Not a long-term solution
- It's physically impossible for me to ask Jake for help.

APRIL 16
2:50 PM

Why Kimberly can't be my assistant manager

I can't afford an assistant manager.

She asked to be the assistant manager.

She's asked more than once.

She thinks we need monthly staff meetings and performance reviews.

She thinks David Sedaris is a "humorless twerp."

She already calls me nine times a day for nonsense problems.

Jenny would quit.

Jenny would punch me in the face before quitting.

Steve would think even less of me.

It would become even harder to fire her.

APRIL 16
4:52 PM

New solutions
> Sell the store
> Promote Steve to manager and get a full-time job

Problems with new solutions

SELL THE STORE

- No one would buy it
- Even if I found a buyer, it would take months
- I'd barely break even

PROMOTE STEVE TO MANAGER AND GET A FULL-TIME JOB

- Steve probably doesn't want the job
- I can't pay Steve enough to make it worth his while
- The only job I'm qualified to do is teach, and it's mid-year

Question
> What the hell does "worth his while" mean? What's Steve's "while"?

Answer
> Oh, it's time. "While" is time. It's not worth his time. Duh.

APRIL 16
8:35 PM

The only times when you're allowed to leave a voicemail
Someone has unexpectedly died
You just won the lottery
Bruce Springsteen would like to speak to you
I'm calling from the future with information that can save
the world

APRIL 17
4:30 PM

Words Steve said today
"Your father came into the store."
"*He said* he was your father."
"He wanted to talk to you."
"He acted like I was lying when I said you weren't here."
"He bought a greeting card and a copy of *The Martian* and
Something Missing."
"He looked nervous."
"Flannel shirt, I think. Jeans. Why?"
"Do you guys talk?"
"He left this for you."

Possible reasons Dad came to the store
Needs money
Angry
Guilty
Dying

Possible things to say if I see Dad

"Nice flannel shirt."

"Why are you here?"

"No, I called you last. I left a message. You never called back."

"I think we both probably suck."

"Sometimes it's just easier to do the stupid thing than to do the hard thing."

"I'm sorry."

"Are you sorry?"

What I wish I could say to Dad

"I was a kid. I wasn't supposed to be the one to hold things together. You were."

"Divorce sucks, but I didn't divorce you. Mom did."

"Do you know how hard it is to call your father when you're not sure if he really loves you?"

"Why?"

What I really wish I could say to Dad

"I wish I could be a little boy again, and I wish you could be my dad, because that loss will hurt me forever."

APRIL 17
5:15 PM

Level 2:	Volkswagen Bug
Level 3:	Corvette (under car cover)
	Subaru Outback (green)

Questions
1. If I said that I'm not doing it, why am I still inventory-
    ing the parking garage?
2. Is this how fatherhood works? If you're not physically
    attached to the baby, the halo effects of the baby are
    temporary?
3. I'm still not doing it. Right?

APRIL 17
11:15 PM

Reasons for fighting with Jill tonight
    She told my father about the baby.
    She told my father about the store (he knew already).
    She told my father that he should go see me.
    She was the reason my father showed up at the store.
    I'll never know if he wanted to see me or was guilted into
        trying to see me.

Reasons Jill called my father
    "You're going to be a father."
    "Enough is enough."
    "Men are stupid."
    "It's my kid too, and I want it to know its grandfather."
    "I couldn't stand the thought of him suddenly dying and
        you regretting not seeing him for the rest of your life."

Addition to "Things that are bullshit"
    "Enough is enough" as a valid argument

APRIL 18
4:30 AM

Additions to Dan's Laws of the Universe

Wanting to be a better human being and finding a way to become a better human being are two very different things.

"Acknowledging the problem is the first step in solving it" is only spoken by people who have actually solved their problems. I bet that plenty of people acknowledge their problem, never solve it, and therefore never say that dumbass thing about first steps.

APRIL 19
6:40 AM

Reasons I'm telling Jill about my on-again, off-again, I'm-not-sure-again plan

If I tell her, I won't be able to do it.

It won't solve the problem, but I won't be alone anymore.

I would want to know.

I think I would want to know.

Jill is smarter than me and might have a solution.

She loves me. I need to believe that.

I can't have a child and this secret. Those two things are too big. I only have room for one.

APRIL 19
9:15 AM

Reasons I didn't tell
    Jill wasn't feeling well.
    I need Harry's mushroom-and-onion pizza and her favorite
        iced tea on hand.
    I'm still afraid to lose her.
    Timing is everything.

APRIL 19
9:22 AM

Addendum to Reasons I didn't tell
    I want to do it even though I know I shouldn't and won't.

APRIL 20
2:15 AM

911
    1. Don't move Jill from bed
    2. Don't move at all
    3. Turn on porch light or open garage
    4. Unlock front door
    5. Lock Clarence in bathroom
    6. Clear way for stretcher
    7. Keep calm
    8. Jill. Keep Jill calm.
    9. Five minutes or less

No

    I can't lose them.

APRIL 20
3:10 AM

Ambulance ride

    Crowded

    No authenticity in the back of an ambulance. Everyone is
        way too positive.

    "Okeydokey" said three times

    Three tries for IV

    Didn't drive fast enough

APRIL 20
4:50 AM

To do

    Stay calm

    Everything is fine

    Try to be as calm as Jill

    Write down everything the doctor says (maybe record?)

    Call Steve to cover me (later)

    Call Jill's principal (later)

    Shit. Let Clarence out of bathroom

    Wash bloody sheets

    Find a ride home when we're all done here

Additions to Dan's Laws of the Universe
> Time stands still at the hospital.
> The worst thing about the hospital is that you're never the
> sickest person at the hospital, so you go from the abso-
> lute sickest person at home or in the ambulance to not
> even close, so you're never the priority and always feel
> shitty for wanting to be the priority.

APRIL 20
5:03 AM

Where is Jill?
What is happening to Jill?
I peed and now my wife is missing.
I also checked my email. And sent an email. But I wasn't
> gone but five minutes.
Fucking beds on wheels.

APRIL 20
5:45 AM

Things I don't understand
> Placental abruption
> Uterine lining
> Gestation
> Fetal heart rate abnormalities
> Partial tear
> Corticosteroids
> Premature labor

What I do understand
>   There are a lot of doctors here now.
>   The doctors look worried.
>   The doctors should fucking hide their worry.
>   I'm afraid.
>   I need to hide my fear.
>   Jill is terrified.
>   Jill might be the sickest person now.
>   I can't lose Jill.
>   We can't lose our baby.

APRIL 21
3:20 AM

Worst Things Ever
>   Waiting
>   Not knowing
>   Not existing

APRIL 21
6:07 AM

Mistakes made
1. Not calling for an ambulance right when the bleeding began
2. Shouting at nurse
3. Shouting at the other nurse
4. Shouting, "Where's my fucking wife?"

5. Allowing the doctor to continue to explain when I couldn't hear anymore
6. Forgetting to call Jill's boss
7. Forgetting about Clarence (should've called Scott and Steph)

APRIL 21
8:40 AM

Update

Blood test and ultrasound positive

"Positive" means the baby is okay (they should fucking say that up front)

Goal is "to get to at least 30 weeks"

Hospital for the duration of the pregnancy

Constant bed rest

IV required

C-section when time comes

What I heard

I will be in constant fear until the baby is born.

APRIL 21
8:50 AM

Placental abruption (according to Mayo Clinic via Google)

- Placental abruption occurs when the placenta partially or completely separates from the inner wall of the uterus before delivery.

- This can decrease or block the baby's supply of oxygen and nutrients and cause heavy bleeding in the mother.
- Placental abruption often happens suddenly. Left untreated, it endangers both the mother and baby.

Bad shit that can happen because of a placental abruption

FOR THE MOTHER, PLACENTAL ABRUPTION CAN LEAD TO:

- Shock due to blood loss
- Blood-clotting problems
- The need for a blood transfusion
- Failure of the kidneys or other organs resulting from significant blood loss
- Rarely, when uterine bleeding cannot be controlled, hysterectomy may be necessary

FOR THE BABY, PLACENTAL ABRUPTION CAN LEAD TO:

- Restricted growth from not getting enough nutrients
- Not getting enough oxygen
- Premature birth
- Stillbirth

Stillbirth (because they keep using words that I'm don't entirely understand)

"The birth of an infant that has died in the womb (strictly, after having survived through at least the first 28 weeks of pregnancy)"

Addition to Dan's Laws of the Universe
Stillbirth has a top 10 worst definitions ever.

APRIL 21
9:25 AM

Update
- Jill would rather push a baby through her vagina than have it popped out of her abdomen by a doctor and somehow blames herself for not being able to deliver vaginally.
- Jill's parents coming day after tomorrow
- Clarence somehow held it until Scott walked him (so not a complete asshole)
- Steve running store
- Kimberly pissed (texted me already)
- There is a Friendly's on the first floor of the building across the street

Addition to Dan's Laws of the Universe
The more a man gets to know a woman's vagina, the more mysterious it becomes.

APRIL 21
9:45 AM

Baby survival rates
23 weeks: 20–35%
24–25 weeks: 50–70%
26–27 weeks: 90%

Addition to Dan's Laws of the Universe
The Internet is a hellscape when it comes to medical information.

APRIL 21
10:07 AM

Update
Our baby is 24 weeks old.
I had to ask.

APRIL 21
2:15 PM

Mom's visit
1. Assumes all doctors are hiding something
2. Assumes all nurses hate her (most do)
3. "How is there no Starbucks in this hospital?"
4. "Everything happens for a reason."
5. "Jake was easy-peasy, but, Dan . . . you fought me every step of the way. I pushed for hours. I was a saint that day."
6. Angry when I can't answer a medical question
7. "Why can't they give you a better room?"
8. "You can't do this all yourself. You should put Clarence in a kennel." (to me only)
9. "Not happening." (I can't believe I said that)
10. "What happens to your insurance when Jill is out of work?"

Addition to "Things that are bullshit"
"Everything happens for a reason."

APRIL 21
4:20 PM

Things to do
Find out what happens to Jill's insurance when she is out
of work
Bring stuff on Jill's list to hospital
Plan for Passover in the hospital (surprise Jill)
Arrange for Scott or Steph to walk Clarence every afternoon

APRIL 21
11:15 PM

New concerns
1. Jill's disability (40 days) plus sick days (126) will expire
in 166 days (November 29)
2. Jill's health insurance will expire on November 29.
3. The promised 12–24-month maternity leave is impossible now.
4. The promised 12–24-month maternity leave was never
really possible (and I didn't realize it until just now).
5. Unless Jill commits to returning to work on September 1,
which will be impossible, we lose our health insurance.
6. None of this is financially feasible.
7. I'm fucked. We're fucked. Jill just doesn't know it yet.

APRIL 22
6:05 AM

Changes with Jill in hospital
  Front door left unlocked overnight
  Nightmares
  No lights left on in empty rooms
  Quiet
  "Last one out of the bed makes the bed" no longer applies
  Clarence slept on the bed
  I ate in bed

APRIL 22
11:30 AM

Letter from the Bill & Melinda Gates Foundation
  No check enclosed
  "Thank you for writing . . ."
  "We are not in the position to grant to individuals"
  "You may wish to visit United Way's free and confidential
      service across North America at . . ."
  "We wish you the very best."

Thoughts
  They actually wrote back to me.
  It was a long shot.
  It's incredible how long shots can start to feel less long
      when you're in trouble.
  I honestly thought I'd get something for my initiative.

APRIL 22
11:50 AM

Why parallel parking is bullshit
1. It's a public performance.
2. It's expected that you can parallel park well.
3. Even though it's expected, people watch you do it.
4. If you succeed, no one gives a damn.
5. If you fail—or even need to adjust slightly—you're a moron who no woman should ever have sex with again.
6. No one cares that your wife's and baby's lives are in danger and you're running out of money and just trying to get a good spot so you can see your wife. You're still expected to be able to parallel park effectively on the first try.

APRIL 22
2:00 PM

Jill
 Relaxed
 Fragile
 Tired

Jill's words
 "I can't believe I'm going to be here for weeks."
 "You need to be nice to Clarence."
 "Your shirt is on inside out."

"I need more snacks. I made a list."

"Please keep your mother away from me as much as possible."

"I don't mind you sleeping at home, but they can put in a cot if you want to stay any nights."

"Work. Run the store. You work, and I'll keep this baby alive."

Steve To-Do List

Bank deposit procedure

Book rep calendar

Checkbook

Duplicate keys

Fire Kimberly

Additions to Dan's Laws of the Universe

The person who has nothing in life except the desire to be the boss is the last person who should be the boss.

Claiming that your inside-out polo shirt is an intentional fashion decision will never be believed.

APRIL 22
5:00 PM

Level 2:	Volkswagen Bug (less dust?)
Level 3:	Corvette (under car cover)
	Subaru Outback (green)

Notes

1. The dustcover on the Corvette makes it the best choice by far.

2. I'm still not doing it but am apparently planning as if I'm doing it.

APRIL 22
5:20 PM

How I trick myself into shoveling the snow in my driveway
1. I'll just do the stairs.
2. I'll just do the stairs and enough to get one car out.
3. I'll do the stairs and enough to get one car out and the bottom of the driveway.
4. I might as well do the whole thing now.

How shoveling the snow in my driveway and planning this plan are alike
They are a lot alike.

APRIL 23
2:30 PM

Best things about Barbara and Gerry (Jill's parents)
1. Never cared that I wasn't Jewish
2. Never mention Peter
3. Laugh when I poke fun at Jewish holidays
4. Text messages are always properly punctuated
5. They know that my mother is a little crazy
6. They know that my brother is a bit of an asshole

7. They think that applauding at the end of a fireworks show is stupid
8. They would never think of spending a holiday at a 5K road race

Slightly less appealing but otherwise endearing parts of Barbara and Gerry

1. Their insistence of a full account of every one of my medical or proposed medical procedures, regardless of how trivial the procedure may be
2. Their reverence for the morning-after-the-visit breakfast of bagels and lox (necessitating an overnight stay when I could've just as easily driven home the night before)
3. Their need for gifts to be opened as absolutely soon as possible (once before I even removed my coat)

Genuinely unappealing parts of Barbara and Gerry

1. Their dogs are small, loud, and have no respect for needs of others
2. Their dogs make Clarence look like a fucking saint
3. They drink milk
4. They do not travel light
5. They prefer written directions to a GPS
6. They live 5 hours away

The problems with Jewish holidays

- Scheduled on their own Jewish calendar so no one (including the Jews) knows when the next holiday is happening until you're weeks (or days) away

- Temple services last for hours
- Holidays last 3–8 days, which is ridiculous and un–American
- No decorations of any kind
- Constantly remind non-Jews that their one appealing and possibly universally celebrated holiday (Hanukah) is a minor holiday at best
- There are at least three correct spellings for Hanukah/Hanukkah/Chanukah
- There are at least three correct spellings for a minor holiday
- Shrouded in guilt
- One of them requires you to read a book at the dinner table before eating
- Overhyped, often terrible food

Overly hyped Jewish food

Gefilte fish (no one actually eats this)
Matzo ball soup (chicken broth with a dumpling)
Kugel (noodle pudding, which should say it all)
Brisket (nothing more than pot roast)
Hamantash (cookies)
Charoset (sweet dark-colored paste made of fruits and nuts, which should say it all)

Addition to Dan's Laws of the Universe

If a food is not readily available in restaurants, it is not a good food.

APRIL 23
8:05 PM

What Barbara said outside the elevator

"Jill is more afraid than she'll say."

"I know this is hard to hear, but losing Peter makes this even scarier for her."

"I want to know everything at every minute until this baby is born."

"Bring the nurses food. They're the ones who keep this place running."

"Forget Passover. I don't like it very much anyway."

"I love your brother, but he makes a lot of things about himself."

"There is no other man who I would want with my baby girl right now more than you."

"I wish you wouldn't wear sweatpants so often."

"Why can't Gerry just get the car without making it such a production?"

APRIL 24
2:15 AM

The worst people in the world

- Families who think holidays are best spent running in early morning Turkey Trots, Ugly Sweater Runs, Snowflake Shuffles, Jingle Bell Jogs, or Ringing in the New Year Runs

- Parents who demand that their children adhere to their own religious beliefs and/or marry within their religion
- Anyone who watches videos on their phones in public places without headphones
- People who back their cars into parking spots
- Anyone who assumes that I want to be called Danny (excluding Bill) (I don't know why)

APRIL 24
4:05 AM

Rules of self-praise
Rule: If you have to say that you were the smartest person in the room, you are definitely not the smartest person in the room.

Jake.

Corollary: Allow others to sing your praise. If you don't feel like you're receiving the credit you deserve, you haven't earned the credit you deserve. Try harder.

Corollary to the corollary: If you engage in self-praise, please know that people will most assuredly disparage you when you are no longer present, including my mother-in-law, outside a hospital elevator.

Addendum to the corollary: Self-praise is permitted in the private company of spouses and significant others, and in job interviews and salary negotiations.

Additional addendum to the corollary: Sarcastic, exaggerated, tongue-in-cheek self-praise is permitted when done to be amusing because humor trumps all.

APRIL 25
5:05 AM

Advice my father gave me that is worth passing on to my child
1. "Shut up and keep swimming." (always spoken in non-swimming contexts)
2. "There's a dozen reasons not to like someone, so don't let the color of their skin be one of them. That's stupid. Just wait until they talk and you'll find a reason."
3. "Wish in one hand, spit in the other."
4. "My house, my rules."
5. "Don't let anyone fool you. Death is hardest on the dead."
6. "What you permit, you promote."
7. "If you're going to be blamed for it, you might as well do it."

Additional advice I know I will offer my child
1. Invest in an index fund immediately.
2. Tighten lug nuts using an actual tire iron.
3. Don't lie to your spouse about money.
4. Harry's mushroom-and-onion pizza and iced tea will always make your mother happy.

5. Fuck people like BJ Novak and James Franco and all their success.
6. Cats are better than dogs.

APRIL 26
9:40 PM

Best parts of my day
    Kimberly's day off
    Dad didn't show up at store
    Felt the baby move
    Jill smiled a lot
    Pie
    "I wish we could have sex."

APRIL 27
11:00 AM

Numbers during doctor's follow-up
    10 fingers on baby
    2 items inserted into Jill's vagina
    10.9 inches
    14 ounces
    ONE full fucking minute before the doctor said the measurements were good
    6 questions related to abdominal fullness, gas, belching, discharge, heartburn
    4 reminders that we don't want to know the sex of the baby

APRIL 27
11:45 AM

Things I do that make me a dick
1. I use the word "sex" instead of "gender" because it's more accurate but really because it makes prudish people uncomfortable.
2. I pretend to be on the phone when passing Boy Scouts selling candy bars outside the grocery store.
3. I assume that people who buy lottery tickets are stupid.
4. I assume that people who scratch their scratch tickets inside the convenience store are the most stupid.
5. I have kept our pending financial ruin hidden from my pregnant wife to preserve my dignity a little while longer.
6. I won't tell Jill that Clarence and I are spooning at night now even though it would make her happy.

APRIL 28
3:00 PM

Jeff Bezos Response
   Return to Sender
   Insufficient Address
   Unable to Forward
   Return to Sender

Addition to Dan's Laws of the Universe
   The addresses of exceptionally wealthy people are apparently not as accurate as the Internet might suggest.

APRIL 29
9:45 AM

Thoughts by Steve

"Three kids bought *1984* today because they saw your Picks of the Month and knew it's on their summer reading list. Have you considered supplying books to schools? Or at least getting your hands on those summer reading lists?"

"I know Hartford Baking Company opened down the street, but maybe they would want to do a satellite location here. To get some coffee and cookies in here. Or maybe do something ourselves. Margins. Right?"

"Maybe we could get some of the poets at the Sunken Garden Poetry Festival to appear here, too? Since they'll be local. Won't cost us anything for travel."

Thoughts by me

I wonder how stupid Steve thinks I am for not thinking of any of these ideas already.

Steve should be running this store.

I need to promote Steve to assistant manager. He'll probably end up paying for his own raise.

Why would someone like Steve even take an assistant manager job?

Added bonus: If Steve does take the job, maybe Kimberly will just quit.

None of this matters because we will run out of money in two months.

APRIL 29
4:45 PM

My "Do Not Read" List
  The Scarlet Letter by Nathaniel Hawthorne
  Ethan Frome by Edith Wharton
  Atlas Shrugged by Ayn Rand
  Anything by James Joyce
  Anything by Virginia Woolf
  The Giving Tree by Shel Silverstein
  The Alchemist by Paulo Coelho (I don't know why everyone
    loves this damn book)

Film versions better than the book versions
  The Firm by John Grisham (ending of the film is far supe-
    rior)
  Forrest Gump by Winston Groom (a truly terrible book)
  The Minority Report by Philip K. Dick (in fairness, Dick's
    is a short story)
  Fight Club by Chuck Palahniuk (good novel, great movie)
  Jaws by Peter Benchley (the Ellen–Brody infidelity drags
    the book down)

APRIL 29
5:20 PM

Level 3:   Corvette (under car cover)
                                  Subaru Outback (green)

Note
> Unless the Corvette moves, it's the one.
> I'm not going through with it, so this is all a mental exercise.

APRIL 30
3:05 AM

Ways our baby is more than just a baby
> A future prom night
> A first word
> Singing Springsteen in the car
> The shock of learning that Darth Vader is Luke's father
> Thousands of hours of reading in bed
> Disney
> Kindergarten recess in the snow
> Hunting for Easter eggs in the backyard
> First steps
> Winter concerts
> Running in bare feet on green grass

Additions to Dan's Laws of the Universe
> A person is more than a person. A person is the promise of everything that person can be.
> A man who doesn't believe in God prays in desperate times in the same way a drowning man attempts to draw breath while underwater. Sometimes all you have left is the impossible.

MAY

Finances
    Savings: 1,020

Income
    A New Chapter: 1,232
    Jill: 2,900

Expenses
    House: 2,206
    Toyota: 276
    Honda: 318
    Car insurance: 175
    Student loans: 395
    Cable and Internet: 215
    Electric: 132
    Oil: 0
    Phones: 180
    Gas: afraid to open bill

MAY 2
5:35 AM

DAYS WITHOUT

Chocolate glazed doughnuts	0
Gum	0
Little Debbie Snack Cakes	3
Flossing	98
Regret over quitting my job	0
Dad	5,818

MAY 2
5:52 AM

MINUTES WITHOUT

Worrying about money	0
Worrying about insurance	0
Panic over baby	0
Fear of future	0
Self-loathing	0

*excluding sleep (except in the case of self-loathing, which
    I am perfectly capable of even while sleeping)

MAY 2
9:05 AM

A New Chapter Picks of the Month for May

Goodnight Stories for Rebel Girls by Elena Favilli and Francesca Cavallo

Turbulent Souls: A Catholic Son's Return to His Jewish Family by Stephen J. Dubner

The Moth Presents All these Wonders: True Stories About Facing the Unknown by Catherine Burns (editor)

Trans-Sister Radio by Chris Bohjalian

The Power of Moments: Why Certain Experiences Have Extraordinary Impact by Chip Heath and Dan Heath

MAY 3
8:15 AM

Things I will never tell Jill

I ate four Little Debbie Snack Cakes in bed last night.

I researched arson using incognito mode.

I coaxed Clarence onto the bed with me.

MAY 6
5:20 PM

Level 3:   Corvette (under car cover)
                                           Subaru Outback (green)

MAY 7
8:25 PM

5 benefits of a closet and/or bureau over a hamper
1. Using items as they were intended makes a lot of sense.
2. Bureaus and closets hide clothing so underwear and jeans do not become constant fixtures of your home.
3. Empty hampers are now available for laundry.
4. Spouses won't feel like ignored jackasses when the clothing sits in hampers for months despite their endless protests.
5. Allowing problems to pile up month after month only creates an eventual breaking point.

Additions to Dan's Laws of the Universe
Putting away a wife's clothing is like smoking crack. Amazing in the short term. Deadly in the long term.
You can make allusions to smoking crack without ever having smoked crack.
Sometimes the benefits of a closet and/or bureau over a hamper can also be applied to the rest of life.

MAY 8
11:15 AM

Steve update
- Summer reading lists acquired from West Hartford, Farmington, Newington, and Bloomfield schools

- $2,042 sale (15% discount) from Northwest Catholic to supply summer reading (Ta-Nehisi Coates's *Between the World and Me*) to freshman and sophomore classes
- I'm looking into One Book, One Town
- Idea (from Jen): "Pop-up bookshop" at JCC book festival (and maybe other events)

Questions
- What is One Book, One Town?
- How do you do a "pop-up bookshop"?
- Is a "pop-up bookshop" what I think it is?

MAY 8
3:00 PM

Hot-water heater
- A thing in my basement that heats water for the house
- A thing in my basement that broke sometime last night while I was asleep
- A thing in my basement that can't be fixed because it's "a dinosaur"
- A thing in my basement that will cost about $800 to replace because when it rains, it pours

MAY 9
8:20 PM

Updated proposed baby names

GIRLS

- Cassidy
- Clara
- Juniper (I can't believe she "kind of" likes it)
- Olivia

BOYS

- Jack
- Charlie
- Noah

VETOES

- Ethel (what was she possibly thinking?)
- Denise (preemptive strike—high school girl who treated me badly)
- Isabella (too many possible nicknames)
- Kindness (Jill says it's even stupider than Cranberry and not a real name)
- Glenn (Jill says it's not a girl's name even though Glenn Close fucking exists)

Addition to Dan's Laws of the Universe

Everything must start somewhere, damn it. Including names that aren't names but are destined to be names.

MAY 10
10:55 PM

Update

Glenn Close is still alive.

Glenn Close is 70 years old.

She's been married four times in four different decades.

The first three marriages lasted three years each.

Currently single

Grew up in a legit cult

Second cousin, once removed, of actress Brooke Shields

Seven-time Academy Award nominee (no wins) (ouch)

Publishes blogs where she interviews other celebrities about their relationships with their dogs.

Seriously.

Born Glenda Veronica Close (not telling Jill)

MAY 11
5:08 PM

Dad's card

The same greeting card that he bought from Steve last week (using my own weapons against me)

- A greeting card is admittedly not a weapon under any circumstances.

No return address. Mailed to me at the store. Fucking camouflaged.

- Probably not intentionally camouflaged, but still, I opened it not knowing what it was.

"I'm not sure why you haven't answered my letters. I can only assume that you're still hurting. If so, that's fair."

Proud of my success with the bookstore. "So happy" for me and Jill on the pregnancy.

"I hope you'll let me see the baby. Someday if not sooner."

"It's hard to be a father, Danny. I know you'll be a better father than I ever was, but it's not easy. I'm not making excuses. Not even asking for forgiveness. I just want you to know that being a father is hard, and I wasn't tough enough. Not brave enough. Not willing to do whatever it took to make sure you and Jake were okay. At least my failure can be a lesson for you."

Sounds so sad. I'm so glad that he's sad because sadness is so much better than indifference.

Says that getting to know Jake Jr. has been a blessing. "A blessing for me, and I hope for Jake, too."

"Men can be mules. Stubborn as hell. It's easy to do nothing, but your Jill opened the door, Danny. I hope you won't close it."

"Be prepared, Danny. Stand strong for your child in a way I never did. Do whatever needs to be done to keep that child safe and happy. Let my failure as a father be my only lesson to you."

MAY 11
5:12 PM

Thoughts

I'm so mad at Jill.

Jill has chosen the perfect time for me to be angry with her. I can't exactly give her hell while she's lying in a hospital bed, trying to keep our baby alive.

I'm so mad at my father.

I love this card so much.

"I wasn't tough enough. Not brave enough. Not willing to do whatever it took to make sure you and Jake were okay."

"Do whatever needs to be done to keep that child safe and happy."

This is the first advice I've received from my father in a long, long time, and it feels so good.

I'm doing it. Dad is right. Whatever it takes. I have no choice.

MAY 12
8:45 PM

Thoughts while Jill sleeps

Making big, daring bets on your future is nothing new. Entrepreneurs do it all the time. Sometimes they go bust. Sometimes they found Apple and Amazon and Google.

It's crazy how confident I feel about this.

Maybe it's all the drugs in here. Osmosis.

I haven't felt confident in so long.

Some people are good at what they do every day. Always confident. I can't imagine.

Maybe it's not confidence. Maybe it's just hope. The absence of hopelessness.

Red from Shawshank Redemption said "hope is a dangerous thing." It can "drive a man insane." But Andy said that "hope is a good thing, maybe the best of things, and no good thing ever dies." I don't know who is right.

Forrest Gump had a similar problem. Do we have a destiny, or is life random? Forrest says maybe both, which is a damn cop-out. It can't be both, dumbass. But Forrest wasn't the sharpest knife in the drawer, so I can forgive him.

Is the baby asleep too?

Do babies dream?

Will *The Shawshank Redemption* and *Forrest Gump* be stupid, old-timey movies by the time this baby is old enough to watch them?

Are babies afraid? Can you be afraid if you only know one thing?

I'm glad the baby doesn't know how much trouble its parents are in.

Why doesn't Jill ever eat her Jell-O?

Why am I worried that a nurse is going to judge me for eating food that wasn't meant for me?

MAY 12
9:30 PM

Idea:

    Run up to a couple on a first date and say to the man, "Listen to me. She's the one. Don't let her get away. I'm from the future. You have to trust me." Then look around like I'm being watched. Turn and say, "I have no time." Then run away.

MAY 12
10:20 PM

Here's what I think:

    Hope is a good thing if you have it, and a dangerous thing if you don't. If there is real, honest-to-goodness hope, Andy is right. "Hope is the best of things."

    But if hope is nothing more than wishful thinking, a pipe dream, Red is right. It will "drive a man insane."

    I have hope now. Real hope. That is why I feel so good right now. Even a bad idea is better than no idea at all.

MAY 13
12:15 PM

Test Run #1 (9 days)

    West Hartford Town Hall auditorium

    Rear exit of stage (unlocked) to hallway (always unlocked?)

OPTION 1: RIGHT TURN TO LOBBY AND MULTIPLE EXITS
(75 STEPS)

- Exits onto back parking lot
  o Metered lot
  o Parking spots within 20 feet of exit
  o Exits onto Main Street and Raymond Road

OPTION 2: LEFT TURN TO STAIRWELL AND SINGLE EXIT
(80 STEPS)

- Exits onto Main Street, West Hartford
  o Church to the right
  o Movie theater, library, shops, restaurants to the left
  o Shops across the street
  o Metered parking on the street

Questions/Problems
1. The police station is two blocks away. Response time will be quick.
2. I can't rehearse the actual robbery.
3. I hate the word "robbery." It's not like that.
4. I suck at improvisation.
5. I suck at confrontation.
6. I suck at aggression.
7. I don't have a gun. I don't want to use a gun.
8. What does a Friday night in West Hartford Center look like?

MAY 14
12:25 PM

Thing I won't ever do

> Send my kid to the dictionary to spell a word
>
> Stare at my phone while my kid is talking to me
>
> Go one day without saying "I love you" to my child
>
> Ride in the back seat with my child like infantilized bubble wrap
>
> Fight with my kid over clothing choices
>
> Force my kid to eat broccoli. Or yams. Fucking yams.
>
> Raise my voice without at least apologizing for being an asshole later
>
> Deny my child ice cream when the temperature exceeds 95 degrees
>
> Allow my child to sleep in my bed on a regular or even semi-regular basis. Never, really. Damn these parents and their kids in their beds.

MAY 14
7:40 PM

My shortcomings

- I have a limited palate.
- I have an unreasonable fear of needles.
- All of my closest friends are the husbands of Jill's friends.
- I don't have any truly close friends.
- I become angry and petulant when told what to wear.
- I can form strong opinions about things that I possess a limited knowledge of and are inconsequential to me.

- I am unable to make the simplest of household or automobile repairs.
- I would rarely change the sheets on my bed if not for my wife.
- I eat ice cream too quickly.
- I procrastinate when it comes to tasks that require the use of the telephone.
- I am uncomfortable and ineffective at haggling for a better price.
- I take little pleasure in walking.
- Sharing food in restaurants annoys me.
- My hatred for meetings of almost any kind cause me to be unproductive, inattentive, and obstructionist.
- Disorganization and clutter negatively impact my mood, particularly when I cannot control the clutter myself.
- I have a difficult time respecting someone's accomplishments if they benefited from economic privilege in their life.
- I leave my credit card at restaurants far too often.

MAY 15
12:15 PM

Dad's letter #1
Written April 1, 2017

I'm sorry.
I'm awful.
Can we talk?

Nine sentences long

MAY 16
3:05 PM

Business Insider's "9 Unfair Advantages That Help People Get Ahead"
1. A need for little sleep
2. Nurturing parents
3. An inclination to optimism
4. A photographic memory
5. Physical attractiveness
6. The ability to resist temptation
7. Charm
8. Connections
9. The ability to selectively ignore people's feelings

My only advantage
    The ability to selectively ignore people's feelings (I think they meant this in a less asshole-ish way than the way it manifests in me)

MAY 17
6:15 AM

Alternatives to a gun
    Knife
    Bomb threat

MAY 17
8:00 AM

I wish
- I was still a below-average teacher with a paycheck and insurance
- I could tell someone about my plan
- Jill and the baby were safe
- I had invested in an index fund 20 years ago
- I had called Dad a long time ago

MAY 17
8:07 AM

People who I would love to tell about my plan if I could, in order
Steve
Bill
Dad
Jill

MAY 18
7:45 PM

Level 3:   Corvette (under car cover)
                                     Subaru Outback (green)

MAY 19
7:10 AM

Bill's phone call

"The phone works both ways, asshole."

Longest pause.

"I'm sorry. Baby shit is scary."

Offered to help in any way possible half a dozen times.

"Fuck bingo. Take care of your wife, numb nuts."

Hartford Baking Company. Tomorrow. 9:00 AM.

MAY 19
11:40 PM

Field & Stream's "Rules of Gunfighting"

1. Forget about knives, bats and fists. Bring a gun. Preferably, bring at least two guns. Bring all of your friends who have guns. Bring four times the ammunition you think you could ever need.

2. Anything worth shooting is worth shooting twice. Ammunition is cheap - life is expensive. If you shoot inside, buckshot is your friend. A new wall is cheap - funerals are expensive.

3. Only hits count. The only thing worse than a miss is a slow miss.

4. If your shooting stance is good, you're probably not moving fast enough or using cover correctly.

5. Move away from your attacker and go to cover. Distance is your friend. (Bulletproof cover and diagonal or lateral movement are preferred.)

6. If you can choose what to bring to a gunfight, bring a semi or full-automatic long gun and a friend with a long gun.

7. In ten years nobody will remember the details of caliber, stance, or tactics. They will only remember who lived.

8. If you are not shooting, you should be communicating, reloading, and running. Yell "Fire!" Why "Fire"? Cops will come with the Fire Department, sirens often scare off the bad guys, or at least cause then [sic] to lose concentration and will. . . . and who is going to summon help if you yell "Intruder," "Glock" or "Winchester?"

9. Accuracy is relative: most combat shooting standards will be more dependent on "pucker factor" than the inherent accuracy of the gun.

10. Someday someone may kill you with your own gun, but they should have to beat you to death with it because it is empty.

11. Stretch the rules. Always win. The only unfair fight is the one you lose.

12. Have a plan.

13. Have a back-up plan, because the first one won't work. "No battle plan ever survives 10 seconds past first contact with an enemy."

14. Use cover or concealment as much as possible, but remember, sheetrock walls and the like stop nothing but your pulse when bullets tear through them.

15. Flank your adversary when possible. Protect yours.

16. Don't drop your guard.

17. Always tactical load and threat scan 360 degrees. Practice reloading one-handed and off-hand shooting. That's how you live if hit in your "good" side.
18. Watch their hands. Hands kill. Smiles, frowns and other facial expressions don't (In God we trust. Everyone else keep your hands where I can see them.)
19. Decide NOW to always be aggressive ENOUGH, quickly ENOUGH.
20. The faster you finish the fight, the less shot you will get.
21. Be polite. Be professional. But, have a plan to kill everyone you meet if necessary, because they may want to kill you.
22. Be courteous to everyone, overly friendly to no one.
23. Your number one option for personal security is a lifelong commitment to avoidance, deterrence, and de-escalation.
24. Do not attend a gunfight with a handgun, the caliber of which does not start with anything smaller than "4".
25. Use a gun that works EVERY TIME. "All skill is in vain when an Angel blows the powder from the flintlock of your musket." At a practice session, throw your gun into the mud, then make sure it still works. You can clean it later.
26. Practice shooting in the dark, with someone shouting at you, when out of breath, etc.
27. Regardless of whether justified of not, you will feel sad about killing another human being. It is better to be sad than to be room temperature.

28. The only thing you EVER say afterwards is, "He said he was going to kill me. I believed him. I'm sorry, Officer, but I'm very upset now. I can't say anything more. Please speak with my attorney."

Finally, Drill Sergeant Frick's Rules For Un-armed Combat.
   1.   Never be unarmed.

MAY 20
12:20 AM

Actual rules of a gunfight that apply to my plan (which won't include a gun)
   1.   Have a plan.
   2.   Have a back-up plan, because the first one won't work. "No battle plan ever survives 10 seconds past first contact with an enemy."
   3.   Flank your adversary when possible. Protect yours.
   4.   Don't drop your guard.
   5.   Be courteous to everyone, overly friendly to no one.
   6.   Decide NOW to always be aggressive ENOUGH, quickly ENOUGH.

Truth
   I may need a gun.

MAY 20
9:20 AM

Bill

Knows the names of every employee at the Baking Company.

"This place is good because it doesn't know it's good."

Knows woman named Rachel who uses this place as her office.

Smiled at the foam heart in his latte. A real smile.

Remembered Jill's name.

I forgot his wife's name (April).

"Is she stressed? Because stress is bad for babies."

Didn't ask if I was stressed.

"A C-section is hard. You'll need to be all hands on deck. No fucking around."

"Henry was born via C-section."

"He was my son."

"He died when he was twelve. Fucking leukemia."

Bill is a Vietnam veteran whose son died of cancer and whose wife was murdered, and he smiles at foam hearts in lattes. How is all of this possible?

"Every day is a blessing. Don't forget that."

I think Bill might actually believe this.

He wants to visit with Jill. I think this is a great and terrible idea.

Additions to Dan's Laws of the Universe

We undoubtedly underestimate people on an everyday basis.

A person who uses a coffee shop as their office is either running away from something at home or sees work as a performative, attention-seeking process.

MAY 20
7:10 PM

Scariest names
    Luther
    Brutus
    Kevin
    Marcos
    Adolf
    Carol
    Butch
    Maurice

MAY 21
4:05 AM

Dad's letter #2
Written July 18, 2016

Building a pergola behind his house
Thinking about retiring
Doesn't attend church anymore
Two cats. Mildred and Olga.

"I want to know you. I want you to know me."
"I'm sorry" three times

MAY 21
5:07 AM

Update

Pergola: an archway consisting of a framework covered with
trained climbing or trailing plants.

I couldn't build a pergola in a million years.

I've never used a saw. Never poured concrete.

Also, I don't get it. Why not build something with an actual
roof?

MAY 21
5:55 AM

Thoughts

I can't build a pergola because my father disappeared from
my life when I was a little boy.

I shouldn't be angry that my father can build a pergola and
I can't, but I am.

Why do we care so much about someone who provided the
genetic material for our existence but little else?

Why do we care so much about someone who we provided
the genetic material for their existence but little else?

MAY 21
7:10 AM

Addition to Dan's Laws of the Universe
You have to admire a person who understands the value of
well-named pets.

MAY 22
9:20 AM

Annoying people
1.   Anyone who insists on reminding us that tomatoes are
     actually a fruit
2.   People who sleep in socks
3.   People who say, "Did you read my tweet?" or "Did you
     read my Facebook post?" instead of just saying their
     tweet or post out loud.

MAY 23
11:45 AM

Stupid baby names
Sarah and Sara (if you have to clarify the spelling for the
     rest of your life, it's a bad name)
Jackson (just call the kid Jack and get it over with)
Mabel (a clear indicator that your parents have too much
     time on their hands)
Stephen (this is the dumb way to spell Steven)

Brandon/Brenden/Braydon/Brayden (no one will ever be
sure what your name actually is)
Clark (mind immediately goes to Clark Kent and Super-
man, which are impossible shoes to fill)
Jenny (the Jen/Jenn/Jenny/Jeni options are just too much)
John (when you care enough to slap the most ordinary
name of all time on your child)
Any name assigned simply to fulfill a familial, cultural, or
religious obligation

Addition to Dan's Laws of the Universe
There is a special place in hell for anyone who thinks they
have any say over the naming of a child with the excep-
tion of that child's parents.

MAY 23
7:00 PM

Jill
She looks so tired even though she's in bed all day.
Hands never leave her belly.
"The nurses loved that blueberry pie you brought. So smart,
hon."
"Are those new jeans?"

Additions to Dan's Laws of the Universe
There's nothing wrong with taking credit for someone else's
idea when it makes a fragile person happy.

Pie is the best food item to gift to others.

When the person responsible for the laundry ceases to do the laundry, one of two things happen:

- A new person begins doing the laundry.
- Clothing emerges from closets and drawers that hasn't been seen in decades.

MAY 24
9:20 AM

Words that belong on a child's T-shirt
- I'm just a kid, damn it.
- This is just a game, jackass.
- Are you really going to rob me of my precious childhood with this meaningless worksheet?
- Leave my coach alone. I don't see you at practice every Tuesday and Thursday night.
- These referees aren't paid enough to deal with assholes like you, so shut the fuck up.
- If some school district in the state declares it a snow day, you'd better damn well call a snow day for us, too.
- Give me $5. It would mean the world to me. It's just another espresso to you.

Possible business idea?
    T-shirt company that puts my wit and wisdom on shirts

MAY 24
11:45 PM

Dad's letter #3
Written July 22, 2016

"I'm so ashamed of myself."

Three sentences long.

MAY 25
7:50 AM

Accomplishments so far this morning
1. Squeezed out (through Herculean effort) last bit of toothpaste from tube
2. Did not get toothpaste on shirt
3. Convinced Clarence that leftover chili was dog food
4. Added dog food to the shopping list
5. Realized that I somehow put on two pairs of underwear
6. Did not become weepy while listening to "Code Monkey"

MAY 25
7:58 AM

Devastating lyrics to "Code Monkey" by Jonathan Coulton
[Verse 1]
Code Monkey get up, get coffee
Code Monkey go to job

Code Monkey have boring meeting
With boring manager Rob
Rob say Code Monkey very diligent
But his output stink
His code not "functional" or "elegant"
What do Code Monkey think?

[Pre-Chorus 1]
Code Monkey think maybe manager want to write god-damned
login page himself
Code Monkey not say it out loud
Code Monkey not crazy, just proud

[Chorus]
Code Monkey like Fritos
Code Monkey like Tab and Mountain Dew
Code Monkey very simple man
With big warm fuzzy secret heart
Code Monkey like you
Code Monkey like you

[Verse 2]
Code Monkey hang around at front desk
Tell you sweater look nice
Code Monkey offer buy you soda
Bring you cup, bring you ice
You say no thank you for the soda cause
Soda make you fat
Anyway you busy with the telephone
No time for chat

[Pre-Chorus 2]
Code Monkey have long walk back to cubicle
He sit down pretend to work
Code Monkey not thinking so straight
Code Monkey not feeling so great

[Chorus]
Code Monkey like Fritos
Code Monkey like Tab and Mountain Dew
Code Monkey very simple man
With big warm fuzzy secret heart
Code Monkey like you
Code Monkey like you a lot

[Verse 3]
Code Monkey have every reason
To get out this place
Code Monkey just keep on working
See your soft pretty face
Much rather wake up, eat a coffee cake
Take bath, take nap
This job "fulfilling in creative way"
Such a load of crap

[Pre-Chorus 3]
Code Monkey think someday he have everything
Even pretty girl like you
Code Monkey just waiting for now
Code Monkey say someday, somehow

[Chorus]
Code Monkey like Fritos
Code Monkey like Tab and Mountain Dew
Code Monkey very simple man
With big warm fuzzy secret heart
Code Monkey like you
Code Monkey like you

MAY 25
9:20 AM

Reasons I seriously worry about Code Monkey in Jonathan Coulton's song "Code Monkey"
His manager doesn't see his talent
He dreams of having everything someday but has no plan
The pretty girl clearly despises him
"Just waiting for now" usually means forever
"Someday, somehow" are wishful thoughts that invariably
    lead to disaster

MAY 25
9:33 AM

Dream jobs
Successful bookstore owner
Statler or Waldorf (in any context)
Best-selling author
Part-time college professor with a full-time salary

Mail carrier
Lottery winner

MAY 26
7:15 PM

I don't have to do this.
I can back out at any moment.
It's crazy.
My wife is pregnant and my baby is in danger and we are
    running out of money.
I don't want to lose my wife.
I don't want to be my father.
I want to be something.
Fifteen minutes will change everything.
It's a good plan.
Maybe I've seen just enough heist movies.
Maybe I've seen too many heist movies.

MAY 26
7:28 PM

Pre-gig positioning checklist
    Car
    Bike
    Duffel

Town Hall checklist
    Door

Ski mask
Door
Stage
Speech
Marcos
Money
Door
Hallway
Ski mask
Door

Escape checklist
Walk
Bike
Car
Car

MAY 27
8:14 PM

This is crazy.
This isn't me.
I can't do this.

MAY 27
8:17 PM

This is a good plan.
We will run out of money in a month.

Maybe I should start a GoFundMe page.

I'm so tired of being afraid.

I'm so tired of waking up every morning thinking about our bank account.

Bill is a Vietnam veteran whose son died of cancer and whose wife was murdered.

"I wasn't tough enough. Not brave enough. Not willing to do whatever it took to make sure you and Jake were okay."

"Stand strong for your child in a way I never did. Do whatever needs to be done to keep that child safe and happy."

There are no other solutions.

This is a good plan.

"Some day, some how" is now.

I'm excited.

I want to be someone.

I can do this.

MAY 27
8:23 PM

Remember

Get between table and audience

Leave ski mask and hat behind before exiting

Speed is more important than getting every dollar

Flank your adversary when possible

Don't drop your guard

Decide NOW to always be aggressive ENOUGH, quickly ENOUGH

Stay calm

MAY 27

8:26 PM

My lines

"Don't move."

"Don't speak."

"If you follow my instructions, Marcos won't have to hurt
    you."

"Drop all the money in this duffel."

"Stay silent."

"Sit still."

"Count to 100."

"I'm sorry."

MAY 27

8:48 PM

You can do this.

These are old ladies.

You can run fast.

This will save us.

This will make it good for Jill and our baby.

MAY 27

8:52 PM

This is the bravest thing I've ever done.

I wish I didn't have to be brave.

I wish I weren't such a failure.

I wish I could just be a regular good man for Jill and our baby.

I am so tired of being a failure.
I want to be someone.
I wish Peter hadn't died.

MAY 27
9:02 PM

Be aggressive.
Move fast.
It's better to get nothing than to get caught.
Remember that these are old ladies.

MAY 27
9:22 PM

This will all be over in 15 minutes.
I need this money.
I'm not a bad man.
I love Jill so much.
I love our baby so much.
Go time.

MAY 27
9:23 PM

"Go time" is such a stupid thing to say.
I'm not a "Go time" kind of guy.
I'm doing this.
I'm doing this now.

MAY 27
9:31 PM

Fuck.

Think.

Can't move until those three guys clear the hallway.

Why are there three guys standing in the hallway on a
    Friday night?

Three suits.

One briefcase.

Arguing about someone named Gary.

If they take the stairs, they will see me.

Hiding under the stairwell was a bad idea. Now I look
    guilty.

If they see me, this is over before it started.

MAY 27
9:36 PM

Who else could be here on a Friday night?

Why didn't I check?

I haven't seen enough heist movies.

One person—politician, secretary, janitor—could ruin
    everything.

I'm so stupid.

MAY 27
9:38 PM

Nothing went perfectly smoothly for Danny Ocean and his
gang, either.

MAY 27
9:39 PM

Bizarre urge to call Bill right now.
Or my father.

MAY 27
9:42 PM

Gary is officially off my potential baby name list.
Fuck this Gary guy. He sounds like a prick.

MAY 27
9:44 PM

Gone.
Elevator.
Now.

MAY 27
9:45 PM

Now.
Now or never.
Don't be Code Monkey.
Go be someone.

MAY 27
9:51 PM

Think.
Breathe.
Don't move.
I did it.
So far.
Will the police check the garage?
Fucking breathe.
Just wait.
Don't do anything stupid.
Think.

MAY 27
9:53 PM

Good
    "Marcos" worked. I can't believe it.
    I was so calm.

I left ski mask and hat behind.

I think I got it all.

Why Marcos worked

1. Scary name
2. The shark in *Jaws* is scariest when it can't be seen.
3. If you are not shooting, you should be communicating, reloading, and running.

Bad

Lady was too afraid to move at first. Started crying. I don't blame her.

I had to yell to get her to move.

I felt way too bad about making her cry.

Police car driving by on South Main as I exited building.

Why did I assume that cops would be at the station on a Friday night?

Old lady definitely didn't count to 100.

Maybe counted way too fast. I should've told her Mississippis.

Old ladies exited front entrance instead of following me to side door.

Old ladies a lot faster than I thought.

Old ladies are smarter than I thought.

70 is apparently the new 50.

I got screwed by my own ageism.

Maybe someone playing bingo saw me. Saw ski mask.

Probably when I yelled.

Old ladies spotted me crossing South Main toward bike.

Probably recognized duffel.

Cops might have spotted me crossing South Main too.

Did they see me turn left and run into parking garage?
Fuck.

MAY 27
9:57 PM

Questions
   Did anyone see me enter parking garage? Cops? Old la-
      dies? Witnesses?
   Did anyone see my face?
   Is it better to leave now or wait?
   Fuck.

MAY 27
10:05 PM

Miracles
   The police cruiser was just past me as I exited the town hall.
   I stayed calm.
   I crossed South Main without getting run over by traffic.
   No bystander tried to stop me.
   Old ladies can't yell loud.

MAY 27
10:07 PM

Waiting is bad.
Circle might be closing.
Other cars are leaving.

Everything seems normal.
I should go.
Drive, Dan.

MAY 27
10:08 PM

Phone
Hospital
Nurse
Stay calm
Been trying to call
Jill in surgery
Baby coming
Don't get in accident driving over
Nothing you can do
Just come

MAY 27
10:11 PM

Plan
Three levels down.
Right onto South Main.
Left onto Sedgwick.
I-84.
Hospital.
Stay calm.
Reread plan.
Drive.

MAY 27
10:12 PM

Fuck.
Line of cars.
Cops checking cars at exit to garage.
Trunks.
Flashlights.
Looking for duffel, I bet.
I'll say, "I went to a movie. Alone."
"Wife having baby."
Stay calm.
God help me.
I'm so stupid.

MAY 27
10:13 PM

Six cars to go
One billion cops
One billion flashlights
One duffel bag

MAY 27
10:14 PM

Four cars to go.

MAY 27
10:15 PM

Don't know any movies playing right now.
Fuck.

MAY 27
10:17 PM

Thank God for the Internet.
No heist movies.
Too bad. Better story.
Story I can never tell.
Still alone. Always alone.
Danny Ocean had 11 or 12 partners. I just want one. Just
  one person.

MAY 27
10:18 PM

Steve. He's the answer. He's always been the answer.
Steve.
Damn it.
This couldn't have occurred to me 30 minutes ago?

Addition to Dan's Laws of the Universe
Solutions to enormous problems have a habit of appearing
  a day late and a dollar short, and in the strangest of
  circumstances.

MAY 27
11:14 PM

My daughter
    Girl
    Born at 10:23 PM
    15.9 inches
    3.05 pounds
    "Big for her age."
    Tears
    "No promises, but it looks good."
    Her father was with the police when she was born.

MAY 28
12:11 AM

Good
    Stayed calm. I can't fucking believe it.
    Pre-breaking Corvette window
    Planting duffel in back seat
    Getting nurse back on phone just before cops inspected car

Bad
    I missed the birth of my daughter
    Duffel still in Corvette (I hope)
    I think I need to return the money

Additions to Dan's Laws of the Universe
    Fathers can't afford to be thieves or failures or fuckups.

Some Laws of the Universe present themselves too goddamn late to be of help.

MAY 28
7:45 AM

Cassidy Peter Mayrock
"How about Peter instead of Alice?"
Didn't plan on saying it. Just came out.
It felt like the rightest thing I did that day.
Jill cried.
I cried.
Nurse liked Alice better.
Bitch

MAY 28
7:55 AM

The truth about Peter
Jill is Jill because of Peter.
I will never be Peter.
I will always be Dan.
I can love Peter because Peter loved Jill.
I can love Peter because Jill loved Peter.
Loving Peter changes everything.
Loving Peter feels right.

Addition to Dan's Laws of the Universe
> The arrival of a baby makes everything seem harder and everything seem easier at the same time.

MAY 28
8:35 AM

Cassidy Peter Mayrock
1. Tiny
2. Beautiful
3. Looks like a fucking genius
4. Looks like an old lady
5. How the hell did the cavemen keep a baby alive without plumbing, garbage disposals, vending machines, and soap?
6. Why do I cry every time I look at my daughter in that little plastic incubator?
7. "My daughter" are the two heaviest words in the world.
8. Somehow, some way, a three-pound bundle of flesh and bone has made everything clear. Wiped away all of my problems and given me a brand-new set of problems. But better problems. The right problems.

MAY 28
10:20 AM

Addition to Dan's Laws of the Universe
> It's easier to be naked to the world when a child is depending upon you for health and happiness.

MAY 28
12:05 PM

Bill

"Wow. You know how to dial a phone."

"Mazel tov!"

He learned "Mazel tov" just for Jill. So he says.

"Peter? Her middle name is Peter? Is that some Millennial bullshit?"

Other "Millennial bullshit" names in Bill's estimation: Sawyer, Dylan, Arlo, Cameron

"I think you did a lot of growing up since I last saw you."

"Your car? Why your car? What's wrong with the coffee shop?"

MAY 28
12:45 PM

What I want to tell Bill

Everything

What I'll really tell Bill

1. I'm running out of money.
2. I robbed a bingo hall.
3. I robbed mostly old ladies.
4. I've never done anything like this before.
5. I hid the money in a Corvette parked in the garage across the street.
6. I want to return the money.

7. I wanted to return the money one second after seeing my daughter for the first time.
8. I need your help.

What I won't tell Bill
1. It felt good to do something well.
2. It felt good to feel brave.
3. A tiny part of me wants to do it again.
4. I'm a badass motherfucker.
5. Kind of.

MAY 28
1:30 PM

19 Questions from Bill
1. Why the fuck are we sitting in the car when a perfectly good coffee shop is sitting in front of us?
2. What?
3. Can you say that one more time?
4. What kind of fucking moron are you?
5. Did you use a gun?
6. Who the fuck is Marcos?
7. That worked?
8. You're serious?
9. Jaws? The fucking shark?
10. How much did you get?
11. You don't know?
12. That's it?
13. Why do you keep writing?

14. Do you have any idea how stupid you are?
15. How do you know the guy who owns the Corvette hasn't found the money?
16. Dust? Your whole plan depends on a layer of dust?
17. What do you expect to do?
18. Why me?
19. Robbing bingo halls is stupid, but now that you have the money, why not keep it?

MAY 28
3:15 PM

Other things I didn't tell Bill
1. I'm more afraid about returning the money than I was while I was stealing it.
2. I almost hope that the Corvette owner found the money so it's out of my hands.
3. Bill is my only real friend.

MAY 28
3:35 PM

Important questions
1. Did the Corvette owner find the money?
2. If so, did he/she alert the police?
3. Did the police find the money?
4. If so, are they watching the Corvette? Waiting for me?

MAY 28
4:30 PM

Bill's plan
1. Gloves.
2. Reacquire duffel.
3. Transfer money from old duffel to new duffel.
4. Write note explaining the situation.
5. Drop new duffel of money into outdoor library book drop.
6. "Now write this down in your little book. In capital letters. IDIOT FUCKING DAN DOES NOTHING AND LIKES IT."

MAY 28
4:40 PM

Letter
   Please contact police.
   Money stolen during the Daughters of the American Revolution bingo robbery.
   Taken in a moment of stupid panic.
   There was no Marcos, so don't arrest some innocent Marcos.
   Sorry.

MAY 28
4:50 PM

Questions
    Will Bill still be my friend after this is finished?
    Do I tell Jill?
    Do I ever tell Jill?
    Do I ever tell Cassidy?

MAY 28
5:10 PM

Worst Things Ever
    Waiting
    Not knowing
    Not existing

MAY 28
5:12 PM

Bill's "You listen to me" orders
    1. Don't tell anyone anything.
    2. Don't do anything stupid.
    3. Don't do anything until I tell you.
    4. Never make a decision unless you have no other choice.
        Waiting is always the best decision.
    5. You need to learn to ask for help, for fuck's sake. Sit
        there and think about that.

6. Make yourself a list of all the shit you could've done instead of committing a felony.
7. Ask yourself why you sit there with a pad and paper or your goddamn phone and make so many lists and then do something so stupid.
8. You're not a bad man. Not even a stupid man. Just a desperate man.
9. Relax. You did the hard part. You stole the fucking money. I just need to return it.

Fucking Hindsight

- Asking Mom or Jake for money is always better than committing a felony.
- Asking Bill for advice is always better than committing a felony.
- Husbands of pregnant wives and fathers of unborn children should not commit felonies.
- Telling your wife the truth is always better than committing a felony.
- That was insane.
- That was also incredible.
- I know why Danny Ocean keeps robbing casinos. It's not for the money.

Addendum

Telling your wife the truth is almost always better than committing a felony except when she was married to a man who was better than you and who died.

MAY 28
5:15 PM

Why I write lists
  I don't want to not exist.
  Not for the world.
  Not for the future.
  Not for my children.
  Not for my daughter.
  I want something permanent.
  Something that can outlast me.
  I want my daughter to always know me.
  I don't want to become my father.
  I don't want to become my father.
  Fuck.
  I write lists so I won't stop existing like my father stopped
    existing for me.
  Fuck.

MAY 28
5:16 PM

Additions to Dan's Laws of the Universe
  Adults spend their lives unwinding their childhood.

  Even when our parents leave us behind, they never really
    leave us behind. They continue to influence everything
    we do, even when we can't see it.

So many of us are Luke Skywalker to some degree, confronting the failures of our parents.

Not existing is just the first of many things to fear from death.

MAY 28
5:30 PM

Contingency plan if Bill is caught
  1. I confess to Jill.
  2. I confess to the police.

If I confess to the police
  I go to prison.
  I lose Jill.
  I lose Cassidy.
  I lose the bookstore.
  Jill and Cassidy have no one to support them.

Addition to Dan's Laws of the Universe
  Sometimes the morally correct decision is not so morally correct when the survival of others is involved.

MAY 28
5:41 PM

New plan
  Call Bill.
  Abort.

Leave the money in the Corvette.
End of plan.

MAY 28
5:42 PM

Reasons why Bill might not be answering his phone
Arrested
Turned off phone
Left phone in car
Saw that it was me so didn't pick up

MAY 28
5:49 PM

He knows I'm waiting. Wondering. Why isn't he an-
   swering?
I allowed an old man to aid and abet in my crime.
What the hell was I thinking?
What the hell does "abet" mean?
Why am I only imagining the worst?
I've made a bad thing so much worse.

Addition to Dan's Laws of the Universe
   Nothing makes a person appear more desperate than plac-
      ing multiple missed calls to another human being.

MAY 28
5:56 PM

Is Bill the kind of person who feels compelled to answer calls and texts immediately, or respond when it's convenient to him?

I am the kind of person who feels compelled to answer calls and texts immediately. This is both depressing and not surprising.

He can't just ignore 14 missed calls even if he's the kind of person I wish I could be. Right?

Addition to Dan's Laws of the Universe
You don't really know a person until you know their personal phone etiquette.

MAY 28
6:02 PM

Truths
I involved Bill because I was afraid.
Not brave.
This is my pergola.
It's a shitty pergola, and I've fucked it up.

MAY 28
6:06 PM

Options
> Wait.

Drive to parking garage and stop him before he recovers the money (if he hasn't already).

Continue to call and text Bill like a crazy person.

MAY 28
6:16 PM

He's been arrested.
The police were watching the car.
I know it.
Of course they were watching the car. Why wouldn't they be watching the car?
Why was it so fucking important to return money to a bunch of lady bingo players?
I can't let Bill go to jail.
I can't go to jail.
Fuck.

MAY 28
6:22 PM

Truths

I wasn't afraid of fighting Jimbo Powers that day. I was
afraid of hurting Jimbo Powers that day.

I'm a conflict-averse people-pleaser. I always have been.

Now I've hurt Bill.

MAY 28
6:24 PM

What I'll say
- Bill didn't know that I was robbing the bingo.
- He called me a fucking moron for doing it.
- His wife was murdered and his son died of cancer and
  he's a Vietnam veteran. You can't arrest him. He's had
  enough.
- It's my fault.
- He was just trying to save a fucking moron.

What I won't say
- He's my best friend.
- He's my only real friend.
- Please don't let me hurt him.

MAY 28
6:27 PM

The phone call

"You owe me $137."

- $100 left behind in Corvette for broken window "even though the insurance company will cover it."
- $33 for new duffel
- $4 for parking

"Yes, I'm okay. Do you think I'd be going over your debt if I weren't?"

"You're right. You owe me a hell of a lot more than $137."

Lecture. *Long.*

Called me (at various moments) stupid, idiotic, dangerous, reckless, a fucking moron, asshole, infantile, ballsy. Also, "You got guts."

"Are you crying?"

I was crying.

"Alone? Who said you're alone? You got Jill. Family. Me. Those folks at your store. You say the stupidest things sometimes."

"What are you doing for money now that you've thrown 20K away?"

"Will he say yes?"

"Go see your wife when it's done, dummy."

"I love you, you stupid, fucking, asinine moron."

MAY 28
7:15 PM

My offer to Steve
    $30K for half of the business (inventory included)
    36 months to pay off debt
    50/50 partnership
    He fires Kimberly

Steve's counter offer
    $20K for half the business (inventory included)
    Immediate cash payment
    50/50 partnership

PLUS . . .

    $5K for half of diaper and thank-you note business
    50/50 partnership
    Immediate payment
    He fires Kimberly

MAY 28
7:50 PM

Luck
    Money still in Corvette
    Bill loves me
    Steve likes me

Left notes/sketches for diaper and thank-you note ideas on
 desk for Steve to see
I didn't end up in jail
Bill didn't end up in jail
Cassidy is tiny but okay
Jill loves me
I figured out a lot of shit

MAY 28
8:40 PM

What I told Jill
 I brought you Harry's pizza.
 We're running out of money.
 I'm not smart enough when it comes to business.
 I'm taking Steve on as a full partner in the bookstore.
 We're also going 50/50 on my diaper and thank-you note
  ideas.
 I'm so sorry.

What I didn't tell Jill
 I robbed a bingo hall of more than $20,000 and then re-
  turned it the next day with the help of an old man who
  I met in the bingo hall who loves me and is my first
  real friend in a long time.

What Jill told me
 "You're plenty smart. Taking Steve on as a partner is brilliant."

"I can go back to work sooner. You don't need to shoulder the whole load."

"We have a daughter and each other. Everything else is bullshit."

"Spend the night here. I'll make room. I want you next to me. We can make out a little."

MAY 28
10:05 PM

21 Truths About Love

1. Real love means always being good enough in the eyes of the person who loves you most but never being good enough for them in your own eyes.

2. One of the best parts of love is the sexy naked rumpus.

3. Holding hands—depending on the circumstances—can be almost as good as the sexy naked rumpus.

4. Love is allowing the most barbaric nature of your loved one to go unmentioned. Even if it means allowing folded clothes to sit in hampers for fucking years.

5. Saying "I love you" for the first time is like leaping off a cliff, hoping to God that she catches you.

6. True romantic love is the willingness to share a toothbrush.

7. People like to say that there are days when you sometimes hate the people who you love the most, but that is fucking bullshit.

8. To truly love someone, you must love the person you never knew, the person you know today, and the person that will someday be.

9. Love does not make everything better, but it makes everything a little easier.
10. We lie to the people we love the most to protect them from the worst parts of ourselves, which is true but also fucking bullshit.
11. Love is the fear that your spouse will die before you and leave you all alone while simultaneously and equally fearing that you will die first and leave your spouse alone. Essentially love demands that you are both killed simultaneously and instantaneously by a small asteroid that you never saw coming.
12. You can't help but love your wife a little bit more when she is topless.
13. Love at first sight is probably bullshit, but love at 19 or so minutes is completely legit.
14. When you send a text that says "I love you" and the response isn't an emoji but actual words, properly punctuated, you know that love is absolute.
15. Love is walking naked through a cold bedroom in mid-January and not worrying that your penis isn't looking its best self.
16. Love means making promises you can't possibly keep and then fighting to the death and the dirt to keep them.
17. "I love you" are three simple words that we whisper to lovers in the dark, say to dogs that don't speak English, cry out during sex, speak to the dead while standing over their gravestones, tell parents before hanging up the phone, and repeat again and again to the people whose lives are gloriously intertwined with our own.
18. There might not be anything more exciting than an unexpected, knock-you-off-your-feet passionate kiss.

19. Loving another person means not needing their best self. Just their real self.
20. Love means that you're allowed to criticize your loved one's most annoying qualities, but if anyone else says even a word about any one of them, you will fucking cut their throats and leave them for dead.
21. Love makes you do the stupidest, bravest, most ridiculous and idiotic things in your life. It makes you scared and crazy and crazed and joyous. Love is all the feelings.

MAY 29
5:40 AM

5 Decisions made while lying beside my wife in a hospital bed in the middle of the night
1. I will tell her about my bingo robbery. Someday, somehow. Code Monkey style.
2. I will tell Bill that I love him.
3. Jill will not go back to work for at least one year. Two if possible.
4. I need to see my father.
5. I need to forgive my father. Someday, somehow.

MAY 29
6:25 AM

Truths
Luke Skywalker forgave his father in the final moments of his father's life, even after his father killed his mentor and

many of his friends and tried to kill his sister. If Luke Sky-walker can forgive his father, I can someday forgive mine.

Star Wars is fiction. Luke Skywalker is not real. But my dad didn't try to take over the galaxy, either. He just stopped calling. I can get over that.

MAY 29
12:10 PM

Bill at the hospital

Brought flowers. Jerk. I haven't brought flowers yet.

"Your husband is a good, strange man."

Sat by Jill. Held her hand while they talked.

"Do you have children, Bill?"

Tears.

Talk of Henry and April.

Tears.

"I'm just doing what everyone I've lost would want me to do. Moving forward. Living life. Making friends with dummies like Dan."

Bill Donovan is a Vietnam vet whose 12-year-old son died of cancer and whose wife was murdered, and he still smiles and cracks jokes and brings flowers to new mothers.

Bill Donovan is a fucking superhero.

Held Cassidy like he's been holding babies his whole life.

Sang "You Are My Sunshine" to my daughter. Son-of-a-bitch can sing, too.

"Bill Donovan, I want you to be my daughter's godfather."

Jill's idea. On the spot.

Tears.

"You just met me. I can't be her godfather."

Tears. Bill and me and Jill.

"Dan gave Cassidy a piece of Peter. I want to give her a piece of you. She deserves as many great men in her life as possible. Stop your crying, old man, and say yes."

My wife is a fucking superhero too.

MAY 29
2:05 PM

Steve's ideas
　　Supplier of books for local schools
　　Partnerships with schools for special student events
　　Writing/art classes with local authors/artists/professors
　　　　(50/50 split)
　　Friday night events (poetry readings, open mics, music)
　　Podcasting booth (rental and maybe our own?)
　　YouTube channel
　　Liquor license
　　Coffee (self-serve carafes until we can afford to build a coffee bar)

MAY 29
9:40 PM

Steve phone call

Stop feeling sorry for yourself. It's annoying.

Needing help is normal. The sooner you understand that, the better.

We should host book clubs in the store.

We don't need to change the name. A New Chapter fits me, too.

Kimberly gave her two weeks.

Don't ask.

We need a bookstore cat.

Heads up: Your wife probably hasn't pooped yet since the C-section. It's going to be a thing.

Thank you for this. It's just what I was looking for.

MAY 30
2:30 PM

Lessons for Cassidy

1. Never, ever ask a woman if she is pregnant.
2. Old people look weird but have lots and lots of good stuff to say.
3. "I'm sorry. I made a mistake. I won't do that again," is always the best first response to any trouble you may be in.
4. Being a parent is hard. Forgive us when we fail you. Forgive us quickly. Please.

5. Most people settle for a career rather than chasing their passion and end up living lives of quiet desperation (not exactly my line). Promise yourself (and me) that you won't let this happen to you.

6. If Uncle Jake says you can't do both, don't listen to him. He's smart and kind, but he's not daring.

7. You don't have to be cool or beautiful to marry the best person in the world. The best people know that looks aren't important and the coolest thing is just being yourself.

8. Remember that almost every disaster will be meaningless in a year. Maybe a week.

9. The unexpected thank-you note is the best kind of thank-you note.

10. The weird ones are the interesting ones.

11. You'll never be as alone as you sometimes feel.

12. "Someday, somehow" is not a plan.

13. Befriend people smarter than you. Older, too. The old ones are the smartest of all.

14. Make sure that your bathing suit is securely fastened to your body before jumping off a diving board.

15. Always record video with your mobile phone in the horizontal position.

16. Your father swears too much. I'm sorry. Don't do as I do in this regard.

17. Never, ever tell a person who asks you how to spell a word to look it up in the dictionary. There is no stupider way to find the spelling of a word. It's also just a dick move.

18. Never, ever allow a person to sit alone in a cafeteria at lunch.

19. Don't be "too cool" to sing, dance, or participate in gym class.
20. Shakespeare isn't as hard as people want you to believe.
21. If you want something, fight for it in writing.
22. Winners arrive on time. Losers are always unexpectedly stuck in traffic.
23. Any chore that takes two minutes or less should be done immediately. Dishes in the sink should never be a thing. Clothing left in hampers is an act of savagery.
24. The single greatest thing you can do to guarantee your future success is to read a lot.
25. Don't ever expect life to be fair.
26. Invest in an index fund. Compound interest is amazing. Reportedly.
27. Complain less than the people around you. If possible, don't complain at all.
28. Nothing good ever comes from watching reality television. Hopefully it won't exist by the time you read this list.
29. Drop mean friends instantly. There are too many good people in this world to waste your time with a selfish jerk-face.
30. Your father will always love you more than you could ever know.
31. Your mother is the best human being on the planet, so treat her well always and love her forever.

MAY 31
2:30 PM

Things I will say to Dad

We're a lot alike. That's our problem.

Let's forgive each other right this very second and forget it
ever happened.

Why a pergola?

I love you. I have always loved you.

Would you like to meet your granddaughter?

JUNE

JUNE 1
6:00 AM

Finances
  Savings: 30,002

Income
  Me: 2,976
  Jill: 0

Expenses
  Mortgage: 2,206
  Toyota: 276
  Honda: 318
  Car insurance: 175
  Student loans: 395
  Cable and Internet: 215
  Electric: 143
  Oil: 0
  Phones: 180
  Gas: 65
  Diapers: 89
  Wipes: 42
  Aquaphor: 19

Boudreaux's Butt Paste (a real thing): 15
Humidifier: 55
Sophie la Giraffe: 27
Nursing bras: 39
Baby clothing: 115
Other stuff: A lot. Babies are expensive.

Number of minutes per hour that I worry about running out of money
    >2

JUNE 1
7:35 AM

Shopping List
    Special K
    Dog food
    Dreft HE laundry detergent
    Ben & Jerry's Chunky Monkey
    Notebook
    Little Debbie Snack Cakes
    Tulips
    Powerball ticket

JUNE 1
8:15 AM

DAYS WITHOUT

Chocolate glazed doughnuts	13
Gum	4
Crying	0
Little Debbie Snack Cakes	0 (fuck it)
Green vegetables	1
Flossing	0
Retail rage	2
Regret over quitting my job	0
Dad	0

JUNE 1
2:00 PM

My *Highlight*'s submission

Not Alone
  First I found love.
  Then I found friendship.
  Then I found me.

  Then she arrived,
  and he returned,
  and I was whole again.

Submitted June 1 by Daniel Mayrock, age 37